*To*
*Our Brave Boys and Girls*
*who have fared forth from their homes,*
*travelling away and away, far further than I could*
*tell you, and twice further than you could*
*tell me, into the Strange Land Be-*
*yond, to push their fortune,*
*THIS BOOK*

# Contents

*Introduction:* Our Folk-Tales . . . . . . . . . . . . . . . . . vii

Billy Beg and the Bull . . . . . . . . . . . . . . . . . . . . . 1

Murroghoo-more and Murroghoo-beg. . . . . . . . . . . . 10

The Queen of the Golden Mines. . . . . . . . . . . . . . . 16

The Widow's Daughter . . . . . . . . . . . . . . . . . . . . 25

Shan Ban and Ned Flynn. . . . . . . . . . . . . . . . . . . 30

When Neil a-Mughan Was Tuk. . . . . . . . . . . . . . . 37

The Black Bull of the Castle of Blood . . . . . . . . . . . 47

The Old Hag of the Forest . . . . . . . . . . . . . . . . . 56

Rory the Robber . . . . . . . . . . . . . . . . . . . . . . . 66

Myles McGarry and Donal McGarry. . . . . . . . . . . . 70

Nanny and Conn . . . . . . . . . . . . . . . . . . . . . . . 84

The Apprentice Thief . . . . . . . . . . . . . . . . . . . . . 92

Manis the Besom Man . . . . . . . . . . . . . . . . . . . . 101

Jack and the King Who Was a Gentleman . . . . . . . . . 108

The Giant of the Band-beggars' Hall. . . . . . . . . . . . 115

# Our Folk-Tales

IN THOSE DAYS Ireland had many Kings and Queens, and was populated by good people. It was not bounded by the sea; all around it was a strange country in which, at rare intervals, arose many-windowed castles inhabited by Giants, Kings, Queens, or beautiful Princesses. On occasions, others are acknowledged; as, when the boy from Ireland fought the dragon, or when his marriage with the Princess was celebrated. The mysterious population which turned up at these times was not whilst he had fared forward on his long and lonely journey, with, at most, a single habitation punctuating each day's progress. Whence, then, this population came, and whither it went, I know not; I never knew; for, no further account is taken of it.

Sometimes the young men of Erin sought adventure in their own land, where were both in plenty. But oftener they went away into the land of mystery, the Country Beyond. They were fearless, these boys, and earned the reward. Some day, long after his kindred had concluded that he was killed or enchanted, the adventurer, maybe, emerged again from the Mysterious Land, with fortune and a beautiful damsel, and with such tales of wonder as set off all the other strapping young fellows who had not yet asked their mother's blessing and gone forth.

Even down to the days of my childhood the Country Beyond still was. Every morning I saw the circle of hills that shut it out. On many, many, bleak and eerie days, when I, herding on our hill, crouched and hugged myself in the cosy shelter of a lone thorn, I watched and watched the rim of those hills, and was filled with wonder, and with longing for the day when I should be able to climb them, and drop into the Land of Adventure. And once in those days, I remember—and the strange sensation is still with me—how, having gone a far journey to the Cormullion uplands after a strayed wether, I saw the tops of the hills of the Country Beyond.

The day came when I did climb, and climb, to the rim, and look over. And lo! the Land of Mystery had vanished. I can feel the ache at my heart even yet. That the land I sought had been there when I was young and innocent, I know. But I had not realised that, year by year, it was melting into the unseen; till with painful suddenness I discovered it was no more.

With us, new folk-tales are being enacted every day. Our Irish boys still rise up and go away to a far land and strange to push their fortune. There are fiery dragons in that land, too, and fell giants, with whom our poor boys struggle sore. There cannot be any princesses there, though; or, the *cailins* at home are better than the princesses abroad; for, when our boys come back with the bags of gold—just as in the stories—they have not damsels also. Jamie Ruadh MacLaughlin of Meenacalliay came back, the pockets of his shop-clothes filled with the gold, and married Rossha MacDiarmuid of the Alt Beag; Myles Griffin of the Haugh, as grand as a king, and every bit as proud, came, and took handsome Grania MacGroarty. I could name a long list of others who did likewise.

In the old folk-tales only our boys went off. But now our poor girls, too, must go. Their mothers cry; and when we are on our knees at night, saying the Rosary, we always pray for the girls and boys who are in the strange land.

Some of them come back again.

Some of them do not find their fortune. They never come. Their mothers in Ireland still cry. The door is open and the hearth bright. If this book happen into the hands of any of these their tears will moisten its merriest page; for, . . . they shall remember . . . They shall remember.

Mary Mother, smooth their rugged road, strengthen their failing hearts, and soften to them the heart of the stranger.

Seumas MacManus

# FAVORITE IRISH
# FOLK TALES

# Billy Beg and the Bull

ONCE ON A TIME when pigs was swine, there was a King and a Queen, and they had one son, Billy, and the Queen gave Billy a bull that he was very fond of, and it was just as fond of him. After some time the Queen died, and she put it as her last request on the King that he would never part Billy and the bull, and the King promised that, come what might, come what may, he would not. After the Queen died the King married again, and the new Queen didn't take to Billy Beg, and no more did she like the bull, seeing himself and Billy so *thick*. But she couldn't get the King on no account to part Billy and the bull, so she consulted with a hen-wife what they could do as regards separating Billy and the bull. "What will you give me," says the hen-wife, "and I'll very soon part them?" "Whatever you ask," says the Queen. "Well and good then," says the hen-wife, "you are to take to your bed, making pretend that you are bad with a complaint, and I'll do the rest of it." And, well and good, to her bed she took, and none of the doctors could do anything for her, or make out what was her complaint. So the Queen axed for the hen-wife to be sent for. And sent for she was, and when she came in and examined the Queen, she said there was one thing, and only one, could cure her. The King asked what was that, and the hen-wife said it was three mouthfuls of the blood of Billy Beg's bull. But the King wouldn't on no account hear of this, and the next day the Queen was worse, and the third day she was worse still, and told the King she was dying, and he'd have her death on his head. So, sooner nor this, the King had to consent to Billy Beg's bull being killed. When Billy heard this he got very

1

down in the heart entirely, and he went doitherin' about, and
the bull saw him, and asked him what was wrong with him that
he was so mournful, so Billy told the bull what was wrong with
him, and the bull told him to never mind, but keep up his heart,
the Queen would never taste a drop of his blood. The next day
then the bull was to be killed, and the Queen got up and went
out to have the delight of seeing his death. When the bull was
led up to be killed, says he to Billy, "Jump up on my back till we
see what kind of a horseman you are." Up Billy jumped on his
back, and with that the bull leapt nine mile high, nine mile deep
and nine mile broad, and came down with Billy sticking
between his horns. Hundreds were looking on dazed at the
sight, and through them the bull rushed, and over the top of the
Queen, killing her dead, and away he galloped where you
wouldn't know day by night, or night by day, over high hills, low
hills, sheep-walks, and bullock-traces, the Cove of Cork, and old
Tom Fox with his bugle horn. When at last they stopped, "Now
then," says the bull to Billy, "you and I must undergo great
scenery, Billy. Put your hand," says the bull, "in my left ear, and
you'll get a napkin, that, when you spread it out, will be covered
with eating and drinking of all sorts, fit for the King himself."
Billy did this, and then he spread out the napkin, and ate and
drank to his heart's content, and he rolled up the napkin and put
it back in the bull's ear again. "Then," says the bull, "now put
your hand into my right ear and you'll find a bit of a stick; if you
wind it over your head three times, it will be turned into a sword
and give you the strength of a thousand men besides your own,
and when you have no more need of it as a sword, it will change
back into a stick again." Billy did all this. Then says the bull, "At
twelve o'clock the morrow I'll have to meet and fight a great
bull." Billy then got up again on the bull's back, and the bull
started off and away where you wouldn't know day by night, or
night by day, over high hills, low hills, sheep-walks and bullock-
traces, the Cove of Cork, and old Tom Fox with his bugle horn.
There he met the other bull, and both of them fought, and the
like of their fight was never seen before or since. They knocked
the soft ground into hard, and the hard into soft, the soft into
spring wells, the spring wells into rocks, and the rocks into high

hills. They fought long, and Billy Beg's bull killed the other, and drank his blood. Then Billy took the napkin out of his ear again and spread it out and ate a hearty good dinner. Then says the bull to Billy, says he, "at twelve o'clock to-morrow, I'm to meet the bull's brother that I killed the day, and we'll have a hard fight." Billy got on the bull's back again, and the bull started off and away where you wouldn't know day by night, or night by day, over high hills, low hills, sheep-walks and bullock-traces, the Cove of Cork, and old Tom Fox with his bugle horn. There he met the bull's brother that he killed the day before, and they set to, and they fought, and the like of the fight was never seen before or since. They knocked the soft ground into hard, the hard into soft, the soft into spring wells, the spring wells into rocks, and the rocks into high hills. They fought long, and at last Billy's bull killed the other and drank his blood. And then Billy took out the napkin out of the bull's ear again and spread it out and ate another hearty dinner. Then says the bull to Billy, says he—"The morrow at twelve o'clock I'm to fight the brother to the two bulls I killed—he's a mighty great bull entirely, the strongest of them all; he's called the Black Bull of the Forest, and he'll be too able for me. When I'm dead," says the bull, "you, Billy, will take with you the napkin, and you'll never be hungry; and the stick, and you'll be able to overcome everything that comes in your way; and take out your knife and cut a strip of the hide off my back and another strip off my belly and make a belt of them, and as long as you wear them you cannot be killed." Billy was very sorry to hear this, but he got up on the bull's back again, and they started off and away where you wouldn't know day by night or night by day, over high hills, low hills, sheep-walks and bullock-traces, the Cove of Cork and old Tom Fox with his bugle horn. And sure enough at twelve o'clock the next day they met the great Black Bull of the Forest, and both of the bulls to it, and commenced to fight, and the like of the fight was never seen before or since; they knocked the soft ground into hard ground, and the hard ground into soft and the soft into spring wells, the spring wells into rocks, and the rocks into high hills. And they fought long, but at length the Black Bull of the Forest killed Billy Beg's bull, and drank his blood.

Billy Beg was so vexed at this that for two days he sat over the bull neither eating or drinking, but crying salt tears all the time. Then he got up, and he spread out the napkin, and ate a hearty dinner for he was very hungry with his long fast; and after that he cut a strip of the hide off the bull's back, and another off the belly, and made a belt for himself, and taking it and the bit of stick, and the napkin, he set out to push his fortune, and he travelled for three days and three nights till at last he come to a great gentleman's place. Billy asked the gentleman if he could give him employment, and the gentleman said he wanted just such a boy as him for herding cattle. Billy asked what cattle would he have to herd, and what wages would he get. The gentleman said he had three goats, three cows, three horses and three asses that he fed in an orchard, but that no boy who went with them ever came back alive, for there were three giants, brothers, that came to milk the cows and the goats every day, and killed the boy that was herding; so if Billy liked to try, they wouldn't fix the wages till they'd see if he would come back alive. "Agreed, then," said Billy. So the next morning he got up and drove out the three goats, the three cows, the three horses, and the three asses to the orchard and commenced to feed them. About the middle of the day Billy heard three terrible roars that shook the apples off the bushes, shook the horns on the cows, and made the hair stand up on Billy's head, and in comes a frightful big giant with three heads, and begun to threaten Billy. "You're too big," says the giant, "for one bite, and too small for two. What will I do with you?" "I'll fight you," says Billy, says he stepping out to him and swinging the bit of stick three times over his head, when it changed into a sword and gave him the strength of a thousand men besides his own. The giant laughed at the size of him, and says he, "Well, how will I kill you? Will it be by a swing by the back,* a cut of the sword, or a square round of boxing?" "With a swing by the back," says Billy, "if you can." So they both laid holds, and Billy lifted the giant clean off the ground, and fetching him down again sunk

---

*A wrestle.

him in the earth up to his arm-pits. "Oh, have mercy," says the giant. But Billy, taking his sword, killed the giant, and cut out his tongues. It was evening by this time, so Billy drove home the three goats, three cows, three horses, and three asses, and all the vessels in the house wasn't able to hold all the milk the cows give that night.

"Well," says the gentleman, "this beats me, for I never saw anyone coming back alive out of there before, nor the cows with a drop of milk. Did you see anything in the orchard?" says he. "Nothing worse nor myself," says Billy. "What about my wages, now," says Billy. "Well," says the gentleman, "you'll hardly come alive out of the orchard the morrow. So we'll wait till after that." Next morning his master told Billy that something must have happened to one of the giants, for he used to hear the cries of three every night, but last night he only heard two crying. "I don't know," says Billy, "anything about them." That morning after he got his breakfast Billy drove the three goats, three cows, three horses, and three asses into the orchard again, and began to feed them. About twelve o'clock he heard three terrible roars that shook the apples off the bushes, the horns on the cows, and made the hair stand up on Billy's head, and in comes a frightful big giant, with six heads, and he told Billy he had killed his brother yesterday, but he would make him pay for it the day. "Ye're too big," says he, "for one bite, and too small for two, and what will I do with you?" "I'll fight you," says Billy, swinging his stick three times over his head, and turning it into a sword, and giving him the strength of a thousand men besides his own. The giant laughed at him, and says he, "How will I kill you—with a swing by the back, a cut of the sword, or a square round of boxing?" "With a swing by the back," says Billy, "if you can." So the both of them laid holds, and Billy lifted the giant clean off the ground, and fetching him down again, sunk him in it up to the arm-pits. "Oh, spare my life!" says the giant. But Billy taking up his sword, killed him and cut out his tongues. It was evening by this time, and Billy drove home his three goats, three cows, three horses, and three asses, and what milk the cows gave that night overflowed all the vessels in the house, and, running out, turned a rusty mill that hadn't been turned before for thirty years. If the master was surprised seeing Billy coming back the night before, he was ten times more surprised now.

"Did you see anything in the orchard the day!" says the gentleman. "Nothing worse nor myself," says Billy. "What about my wages now," says Billy. "Well, never mind about your wages," says the gentleman, "till the morrow, for I think you'll hardly come back alive again," says he. Well and good, Billy went to his bed, and the gentleman went to his bed, and when the gentleman rose in the morning says he to Billy, "I don't know what's wrong with two of the giants; I only heard one crying last night." "I don't know," says Billy, "they must be sick or something." Well, when Billy got his breakfast that day again, he set out to the orchard, driving before him the three goats, three cows, three horses and three asses and sure enough about the middle of the day he hears three terrible roars again, and in comes another giant, this one with twelve heads on him, and if the other two were frightful, surely this one was ten times more so. "You villain, you," says he to Billy, "you killed my two brothers, and I'll have my revenge on you now. Prepare till I kill you," says he; "you're too big for one bite, and too small for two; what will I do with you?" "I'll fight you," says Billy, shaping out and winding the bit of stick three times over his head. The giant laughed heartily at the size of him, and says he, "What way do you prefer being killed? Is it with a swing by the back, a cut of the sword, or a square round of boxing?" "A swing by the back," says Billy. So both of them again laid holds, and my brave Billy lifts the giant clean off the ground, and fetching him down again, sunk him down to his arm-pits in it. "Oh, have mercy; spare my life," says the giant. But Billy took his sword, and, killing him, cut out his tongues. That evening he drove home his three goats, three cows, three horses, and three asses, and the milk of the cows had to be turned into a valley where it made a lough three miles long, three miles broad, and three miles deep, and that lough has been filled with salmon and white trout ever since. The gentleman wondered now more than ever to see Billy back the third day alive. "Did you see nothing in the orchard the day, Billy?" says he. "No, nothing worse nor myself," says Billy. "Well that beats me," says the gentleman. "What about my wages now?" says Billy. "Well, you're a good mindful boy, that I couldn't easy do without," says the gentleman, "and I'll give you any wages you ask for the future." The next morning, says the gentleman to Billy, "I heard none of the giants crying last night, however it comes. I don't know what has happened to them?" "I don't know," says Billy, "they must be sick or something." "Now, Billy," says the gentleman, "you must look after the cattle the day again, while I go to see the fight." "What fight?" says Billy. "Why," says the gentleman, "it's the king's daughter is going to be devoured by a fiery dragon, if the greatest fighter in the land, that they have been feeding specially for the last three months, isn't able to kill the dragon first. And if he's able to kill the dragon the king is to give him the daughter in marriage." "That will be fine," says Billy. Billy drove out his three goats, three cows, three horses, and three asses to the orchard that day again, and the like of all that passed that day to see the fight with the man and the fiery dragon, Billy never witnessed before. They went in coaches and carriages, on horses and jackasses, riding and walking, crawling and creeping. "My tight little fellow," says a man that was passing to Billy, "why don't you come to see the great fight?" "What would take the likes of me there?" says Billy. But when Billy found them all gone he saddled and bridled the best black horse his master had, and put on the best suit of clothes he could get in his master's house, and rode off to the fight after the rest. When Billy went there he saw the king's daughter with the whole court about her on a platform before the castle, and he thought he never saw anything half as beautiful, and the great warrior that was to fight the dragon was walking up and down on the lawn before her, with three men carrying his sword, and every one in the whole country gathered there looking at him. But when the fiery dragon came up with twelve heads on him, and every mouth of him spitting fire, and let twelve roars out of him, the warrior ran away and hid himself up to the neck in a well of water, and all they could do they couldn't get him to come and face the dragon. Then the king's daughter asked if there was no one there to save her from the dragon, and get her in marriage. But not one stirred. When Billy saw this, he tied the belt of the bull's hide round him, swung his stick over his head, and went in, and after a terrible fight entirely, killed the dragon. Every one then gathered about to find who the stranger was. Billy jumped on his horse and darted away sooner than let them know; but just as he was getting away the king's daughter pulled the shoe off his foot. When the dragon was killed the warrior that had hid in the well of water came out, and cutting the heads off the dragon he brought them to the king, and said that it was he who killed the dragon, in disguise; and he claimed the king's daughter. But she tried the shoe on him and found it didn't fit him; so she said it wasn't him, and that she would marry no one only the man the shoe fitted. When Billy got home he changed the clothes again, and had the horse in the stable, and the cattle all in before his master came. When the master came, he began telling Billy about the wonderful day they had entirely, and about the warrior hiding in the well of water, and about the grand stranger that came down out of the sky in a cloud on a black horse, and killed the fiery dragon, and then vanished in a cloud again. "And, now," says he, "Billy, wasn't that wonderful?" "It was, indeed," says Billy, "very wonderful entirely." After that it was given out over the country that all the people were to come to the king's castle on a certain day, till the king's daughter would try the shoe on them, and whoever it fitted she was to marry them. When the day arrived Billy was in the orchard with the three goats, three cows, three horses, and three asses, as usual, and the like of all the crowds that passed that day going to the king's castle to get the shoe tried on, he never saw before. They went in coaches and carriages, on horses and jackasses, riding and walking, and crawling and creeping. They all asked Billy was not he going to the king's castle, but Billy said, "Arrah, what would be bringin' the likes of me there?" At last when all the others had gone there passed an old man with a very scare-crow suit of rags on him, and Billy stopped him and asked him what boot would he take and swap clothes with him. "Just take care of yourself, now," says the old man, "and don't be playing off your jokes on my clothes, or maybe I'd make you feel the weight of this stick." But Billy soon let him see it was in earnest he was, and both of them swapped suits, Billy giving the old man boot. Then off to the castle started Billy, with the suit of rags on his back and an old stick in his hand, and when he come there he found all in great commotion trying on the shoe, and some of them cutting down their foot, trying to get it to fit. But it was all of no use, the shoe could be got to fit none of them at all, and the king's daughter was going to give up in despair when the wee ragged looking boy, which was Billy, elbowed his way through them, and says he, "Let me try it on; maybe it would fit me." But the people when they saw him, all began to laugh at the sight of him, and "Go along out of that, you example you," says they shoving and pushing him back. But the king's daughter saw him, and called on them by all manner of means to let him come up and try on the shoe. So Billy went up, and all the people looked on, breaking their hearts laughing at the conceit of it. But what would you have of it, but to the dumfounding of them all, the shoe fitted Billy as nice as if it was made on his foot for a last. So the king's daughter claimed Billy as her husband. He then confessed that it was he that killed the fiery dragon; and when the king had him dressed up in a silk and satin suit, with plenty of gold and silver ornaments everyone gave in that his like they never saw afore. He was then married to the king's daughter, and the wedding lasted nine days, nine hours, nine minutes, nine half minutes and nine quarter minutes, and they lived happy and well from that day to this. I got brogues of *brochan**  and breeches of glass, a bit of pie for telling a lie, and then I came slithering home.

---

*Porridge.

# Murroghoo-more
# and Murroghoo-beg

MURROGHOO-MORE and Murroghoo-beg were cousins and
lived in the one townland. Murroghoo-more was the
biggest and strongest and always kept poor Murroghoo-beg at
his command, and made him do what he liked. Murroghoo-
more one day gave Murroghoo-beg a skillet and says he to him,
"Murroghoo-beg, go out to the wood and pluck the full of that
skillet of raspberries." Murroghoo-beg took the skillet and went
to the wood and filled it with the raspberries, but on the way
home again there come on a shower, and Murroghoo-beg had to
go in under a bush till it would pass over. When he was in under
the bush he began to take the hunger, and when he looked at
the fine skillet of ripe raspberries he was carrying home to lazy
Murroghoo-more his teeth began to water, and poor
Murroghoo-beg couldn't help tasting one raspberry just to see
what they were like, and then another, and another, till at last he
finished the skillet. Very well and good. When he came home,
says Murroghoo-more, "Where's the raspberries I sent ye for?"
"I had the full of the skillet, but hunger took me on the road
home, and I ate them," says Murroghoo-beg. So Murroghoo-
more thrashed him soundly. Well the next morning Murroghoo-
more come to Murroghoo-beg again, and gave him the skillet,
and told him to go to the wood and pull him a skillet of raspberries; "and mind," says he, "that hunger doesn't take you on
the way home the day, or it will be worse for ye." Poor
Murroghoo-beg promised that it would not, and he set out this
day again and pulled the full of the skillet of raspberries in the
wood; and on his way home doesn't a shower come on again and

put him under a bush, and the hunger took him again, and he ate the skillet of raspberries. So when he went home Murroghoo-more asked him where was his raspberries, and poor Murroghoo-beg told him again what happened to him. "All right," says Murroghoo-more, and he set to and thrashed Murroghoo-beg soundly. Very good, the next morning Murroghoo-more comes to Murroghoo-beg the third time, and gave him the skillet and told him to go out to the wood and pull him a skillet of raspberries, and that if he ate the raspberries this time again he would surely have his life. But poor Murroghoo-beg ate a hearty breakfast, and said there was no fear of the hunger taking him the day. So out he goes to the wood and fills his skillet again, and set out whistling to carry it home to Murroghoo-more. But what would you have of it but the shower put Murroghoo-beg anunder the bush, and the hunger took him and he ate the skillet of raspberries again. Then he went home to Murroghoo-more, and says Murroghoo-more, "Where's my skillet of raspberries I sent you to the wood to pluck for me." "Och!" says Murroghoo-beg, says he, "the hunger took me and I ate them." "All right," says Murroghoo-more, "ye must die. I'll pick out your eyes first, and then I'll leave it to yourself to choose how to die after." So he got a pointed stick, and setting it on fire, he put it into poor Murroghoo-beg's eyes and burned them out. "Now," says Murroghoo-more, "what am I to do with you?" "Well," says Murroghoo-beg, says he, "I suppose the easiest death will be to leave me over in that old church all night, for no one that stops a night there is ever alive in the morning." Very well and good, Murroghoo-more took poor Murroghoo-beg over to the old church and left him there. About midnight poor Murroghoo-beg hears the roolie-boolie and helter-skelter, and in comes a whole rajimint of cats. Murroghoo-beg got under some planks in the corner, so he wasn't seen, but could hear all the cats would say. After a lot of chat they proposed to tell stories. So they squared themselves round, and then they differed on which of them would tell the first story. Every one of them put it to an older one till at length it came to an old granny cat, and she consented to tell her story, but she said the house would have to be well searched first, for it wouldn't do for anyone to overhear what she had to say. Well and good, all the young cats went hurry skurry round the church, looking under the seats and everywhere, and poor Murroghoo-beg begun to tremble in his skin now with fear of being caught, for he knew they would tear him to pieces. But the young cats were in such a hurry to hear the old granny cat's story that they forgot to look under the planks where Murroghoo-beg was hid. Then they reported there was no one in the house nor round about it, so the old cat begun her story.

"Well," says she, "the daughter of the king is lying bad, and very bad, and she has been that way now, off and on, for twelve months, only it's what it's worse she is getting every day, and all the first doctors in the land have been called in, and the king has offered her weight in gold to the man that will cure her, but it's all of no use. None of them can make out what's wrong with her, or how she can be cured. But I know her complaint and know how to cure it, and I'll tell you it all, only you must promise never to come out with it, for I mean to let her die a lingering death," says she.

They all promised that they'd never split lips again on the subject, so the spiteful old cat went on——

"Well, then," says she, "long ago, when she was a child, she saw me putting my head into a noggin of sweet-milk, and she came up and hit me on the head, and made me drop the mouthful I had got, back into the pail again, and she then took a drink out of the pail herself with the venom of my spittal in it, and from that day young serpents have been growing in her. There's one thing, and only one, would cure her, and rid her of the serpents, and that, please the devil, she'll never have, nor never know of—that is, just three spoonfuls of water out of the well here at the back of the church, to be taken nine mornings on the bare stomach, fasting."

Murroghoo-beg heard all this, and he waited till the cats went all away, and in the morning he came out, and, groping his way to the well, he took off his boots and filled one of them with water, and then started for the king's palace, and when he came there all that place was in a commotion with all the first doctors of the three kingdoms and France besides. And when poor

Murroghoo-beg come in, and he was asked what was wrong with him, and he said he had come to cure the king's daughter; and they asked him where was his medicine, and he said he had it in his boot, they commenced laughing at him, and the doctors ordered him to be turned out. And the servants begun to shove and push poor Murroghoo-beg to put him out of the palace, but Murroghoo wasn't for going, and that was the roolie-boolie! And by the toss o' wars what with the wrestling and the fighting and the racketing they made, doesn't the sick lady hear it, and she sent down word to know what was going on. And they sent back the word that it was a poor demented man that wanted to cure her ladyship with a bootful of spring water. "Let him come up," said her ladyship; "sure he can't do no worse nor the rest of them anyhow." Well, her wish, of course, was a command. Up my brave Murroghoo-beg was taken, and when he come into her ladyship's presence he told her he would get her out of bed in short time. So he put her under cure of three spoonfuls of the water he had in his boot, on the bare stomach fasting for nine mornings. The other doctors looked on and shook their heads, but daren't say anything. But the tables were soon turned on them, for sure enough the very first day she took the water she felt great ease entirely, and so on day after day, till on the morning of the ninth day after she had took the medicine she was taken with a fit of vomiting, and vomited up the full of a basin of young serpents, and then she got up out of her bed, and walked out as fine, strong, and handsome a young woman as you would ask to see. And she was so well pleased at this, and the king was so well pleased that they sent home Murroghoo-beg with double her weight in gold along with him. After Murroghoo-beg came home he went to the well behind the old church for nine mornings bathing his eyes in it every morning, and on the ninth morning his eyes and his eyesight were as good as ever. Poor Murroghoo-beg could now live happy and well for the remainder of his days, only the dread was in him still of Murroghoo-more, and he knew that when Murroghoo-more would hear of his good luck he would put him to death, and take his gold. And right enough it wasn't long till it come to Murroghoo-more's ears that Murroghoo-beg was back alive

again with his eyes and eyesight, and no end of gold into the bargain, however he had come by it. So my brave Murroghoo-more
starts out and comes to Murroghoo-beg, and, "Murroghoo-beg,"
says he, "I thought I left ye for death; and is it here ye are now?"
"Oh," says Murroghoo-beg, "but it was you that did me the good
turn entirely. Here I am now with eyes and my eyesight, and a
good bag of gold into the bargain; and if you would only put out
my eyes and leave me overnight in the old church again, I think
I would have still better luck this time." "How is that?" says
Murroghoo-more. "Why," says Murroghoo-beg, this is the way
of it"—and he commences telling Murroghoo-more about how
there was a lot of cats came every night to the old church, and
commenced to tell stories every one of them about where there
was no end of treasure hid, and about wonderful easy cures for
eyes that would be picked out of men's heads, till he had
Murroghoo-more beside himself with delight. "You must take
and pick out my eyes, now," says Murroghoo-more, "and leave
me in the old church the night." "Very good," says Murroghoo-
beg, "I'll do that with a heart and a half." So reddening a
pointed stick in the fire Murroghoo-beg picked out the eyes of
Murroghoo-more, and took him to the old church, and hid him
under the same planks he had been under himself. And there
Murroghoo-more lay till midnight, when he hears the roolie-
boolie starting, and in comes tumbling the cats. "Och, square
round, square round," the young ones begun to cry till we tell
stories. "Now," says Murroghoo-more to himself, "now I'm in
for it." "I'll tell no more stories," says the old granny cat, "for the
last night that I told the story about the king's daughter you
didn't search the house rightly, and Murroghoo-beg was lying
hid there under them planks in the corner, and he heard the
whole rehearsal and went off and cured her—bad luck to him
and her!—and got double her weight in gold for it, and cured his
own eyes that had been picked out by Murroghoo-more into the
bargain." "Oh, but," says the young cats, "we'll search better this
night, and I'll warrant you we'll look under the planks, and may
the Lord pity Murroghoo-beg if he's eavesdropping again." So
off they set at a gallop to search the house, beginning first by
looking under the planks; and when they went in there, oh, that

was the ruction and the uproar, and out they comes, hauling Murroghoo-more with them, and when the old cats saw this they come bouncing down, spitting, and their eyes flashing fire, and all of them fell on him, tearing him to pieces, and it was trying to see who would get most of him they were. So, when Murroghoo-beg went to the old church in the morning to see what had become of Murroghoo-more, he got nothing only a rickle of bare bones. Murroghoo-beg buried these, and went home and lived happy ever after.

# The Queen of the Golden Mines

ONCE ON A TIME there was a King of Ireland, and he had three sons, Teddy, Billy, and Jack. Teddy and Billy was the two eldest, and they were brave able boys. But Jack was the youngest, a *gauchy, dawnie* sort of a lad that was good for nothing only feeding fowls and doing odd turns about the house. When they grew up to be men, Teddy and Billy one day said they'd go away to travel and see the world, for they'd only be good-for-nothing omadhauns if they'd stay here all their lives. Their father said that was good, and so off the both of them started. And that night when they halted from their travelling, who does they see coming up after them, but Jack; for it seems he commenced to think *long*, when he found them gone, and he was that lonesome that he couldn't stay behind them. And there he was dressed in his old tattered clothes, a spec-*tacle* for the world, and a disgrace to them; for of course, they were done off with the best of everything—rale gentlemen, as becomed their father's sons. They said to themselves they'd be long sorry to let that picthur with them—for he *was* a picthur, and no doubt of it—to be an upcast to them wherever they'd go. So before they started on again next mornin' they tied Jack to a millstone, and left him there. That night again, when they went to stop from their travellin', what would you have of it but there was me brave Jack once more, not a hundred parches behind them, and he dragging the millstone after him. Teddy and Billy said this was too bad entirely; and next day, before they started again, they tied another millstone to him, and they said, "Well, you'll not get away from here in a hurry anyhow, boy." So on they went again on their journey, laughing and cracking jokes, and telling passages, to pass the time; but that night again, when they went to stop from their journey, lo! and behold ye, who does they see coming tearing afther them but my poor Jack, once more, with the two millstones dragging behind him. Then they were in a quandhary entirely, and they begun to consider what was best to do with him, for they saw there was no holdin' or tyin' of him, or keepin' him back at all, at all, for if they were to tie him to a mountain in the mornin', he'd be afther them with the mountain rattling at his heels again' night. So they come to the conclusion that it was best to take Jack with them, and purtend him to be their hired boy, and not their brother at all. Of course, me poor Jack, that was always agreeable, was only too ready to go on these terms; and on the three of them went, afore them, till at length they reached the King of England's Castle. When the King of England heard Teddy and Billy was the King of Ireland's two sons, he give them *ceud mile failte,* was plaised and proud to see them, ordhered them to be made much of, then opened his hall door, an' asked in the nobility an' genthry of the whole counthry side to a big dinner and ball that he gave in their honour. But what do you have of it, but in the middle of the ball doesn't Teddy have a fall out with the King of England's son, and sthruck him, and then that was the play! The hubbub and *hooroosh* got up, and the King ordhered the ball to be stopped, and had Teddy taken pres'ner, and Billy and Jack ordhered away out of the kingdom. Billy and Jack went away, vexed in their hearts at leaving Teddy in jail, and they travelled away till they came to France, and the King of France's Castle. Here when the King of France heard that Billy, the King of Ireland's son, had come to see him he went out and welcomed him, an' asked in himself and Jack to come in and make a visit with him. And, like the King of England, he thought he couldn't make too much of the King of Ireland's sons, and threw open his hall door and asked in the whole nobility and clergy and genthry of all the counthry side into a great dinner and ball given in Billy's honour. But lo! and behould ye, doesn't it turn up at this ball, too, that Billy had a squabble with the King of France's son and sthruck him, and the ball was stopped by the King's ordhers, and the people sent home, and Billy taken prisoner, and there was poor Jack now left all alone. The King of France, taking pity on Jack, employed him as a boy. And Jack was getting along very well at Court, and the king and him used to have very great yarns together entirely. At length a great war broke out betwixt France and Germany; and the King of France was in great trouble, for the Germans were slaughtering and conquering all before them. Says Jack, says he to the King one day, "I wish I had only half a rajimint of your men, and you'd see what I would do." Instead of this the King gave him a whole army, and in less nor three days there wasn't a German alive in the whole kingdom of France. It was the King was the thankful man to Jack for this good action, and said he never could forget it to him. After that Jack got into great favour at Court, and used to have long chats with the Queen herself. But Jack soon found that he never could come into the Queen's presence that he didn't put her in tears. He asked her one day what was the meaning of this, and she told him that it was because she never looked on him that he didn't put her in mind of her infant son that had, twelve months' before, been carried away by the Queen of the Golden Mines, and who she had never heard tale or tidings of from that day to this. "Well, be this and be that," says Jack, says he, "but I'm not the man to leave ye in your trouble if I can help it; and be this and be that over again," says he, "but I won't sleep two nights in the one bed, or eat two meals' meat in the one house, till I find out the Queen of the Golden Mines's Castle, and fetch back your infant son to ye—or else I'll not come back livin'." "Ah," says the Queen, "that would never do!" and "Ah," says the King, "that would never do at all, at all!" They pointed out and showed to him how a hundred great knights had gone on the same errand before him, and not one of them ever come back livin', and there was no use in him throwin' away his life, for they couldn't afford to lose him. But it was all no use; Jack was bound on goin', and go he would. So, the very next morning he was up at cock-crow, and afther leavin' good-bye with the whole of them, and leavin' the King and the Queen in tears, he started on his journey. And he travelled away afore him, inquiring his way to the Castle of the Queen of the Golden Mines; and he travelled and tramped for many a weary day, and for many a weary week, and for many a weary month; till at last when it was drawing on twelve months from the day he left the Castle of the King of France, one day tors't evening he was travelling through a thick wood, when he fell in with an old man, resting, with a great bundle of sticks by his side; and "Me poor old man," says Jack, says he, "that's a mighty great load entirely for a poor man of your years to be carryin'. Sure, if ye'll allow me, I'll just take them with me, for ye, as far as you're goin'." "Blissins on ye!" says the ould man; "an' an ould man's blissin' atop of that; an' thanky." "Nobbut, thanky, yerself, for your good wishes," says Jack, says he, throwin' the bundle of sticks on his shoulder, an' marchin' on by the ould man's side. And they thravelled away through the wood till they come at last to the ould man's cabin. And the ould man axed Jack to come in and put up with him for the night, and such poor accommodation as he had, Jack was heartily welcome to them. Jack thanked him and went in and put up the night with him, and in the morning Jack told the ould man the arrand he was on and axed if he'd diract him on his way to the Queen of the Golden Mines's Castle. Then the ould man took out Jack, and showed him a copper castle glancing in the sun, on a hill opposite, and told him that was his journey's end. "But, my poor man," says he, "I would strongly advise ye not to go next or near it. A hundred knights went there afore you on the self-same errand, and their heads are now stuck on a hundred spears right afore the castle; for there's a fiery dhragon guards it that makes short work of the best of them." But seeing Jack wasn't to be persuaded off his entherprise nohow, he took him in and gave him a sword that carried ten men's strength in it along with that of the man that wielded it. And he told Jack, if he was alive again' night, and not killed by the dhragon, to come back to his cabin. Jack thanked him for the sword, and promised this, and then he set out for the castle. But lo! and behold ye, no sooner did Jack come anear the castle than a terrible great monsther of a dhragon entirely, the wildest ever Jack seen or heard tell of, come out from the castle, and he opened his mouth as wide as the world from side to side, and let a roar that started the old grey eagle on top of Croaghpathrick mountain at home

in Ireland. Poor Jack thrimbled from head to foot—and small
wonder he did—but, not a bit daunted, he went on to meet the
dhragon, and no sooner were they met than he to it and the
dhragon to it, and they fought and sthrove long and hard, the
wildest fight by far that poor Jack ever entered into, and they
fought that way from early mornin' till the sun went down, at
one time Jack seemin' to be gettin' the betther of the dhragon,
and the next minute the dhragon gettin' the betther of Jack; and
when the sun went down they called a truce of peace till next
day; and Jack dragged himself back to the cabin in small hopes
of being able to meet the dhragon more, for he was covered
over with wounds from head to foot. But when he got to the
cabin the ould man welcomed him back alive, and he took down
a little bottle of ointment and rubbed it over Jack, and no sooner
did he rub it over him that Jack's wounds were all healed as well
as ever again. And Jack went out a new man the next mornin' to
give the dhragon another try for it this day. And just as on the
day afore the fiery dhragon come down the hill meeting poor
Jack; and the dhragon opened his mouth as wide as the world,
and gave a roar that shook the nails on the toes of the great grey
eagle on top of Croaghpathrick mountain at home in Ireland,
and then he fell on Jack, and Jack fell on him, and the dhragon
to it, and Jack to it; and the dhragon gave Jack his fill, and Jack
gave the dhragon his fill; and if they fought hard the day afore
they fought double as hard this day, and the dhragon put very
sore on Jack entirely till the sun went down. Then again they
agreed on a truce of peace till the next mornin', and Jack
dragged himself back as best he could to the cabin again, all covered over with cuts and bruises, and streaming down with blood.
And when he came there the ould man took down a little bottle
of ointment and rubbed Jack over with it, and he was healed as
well as ever again. Next morning Jack was up quite fresh and
ready for another day's battling, and the ould man told Jack that,
win or lose, this day was like to end the battle. And he said if
Jack happened (as God send) to come off victorious, he was to
go into the Castle, and there he would find a great number of
beautiful virgins running about in great confusion to prevent
Jack from discovering their mistress the Queen of the Golden

Mines, and every one of them axing, "Is it me ye want? Is it me ye want?" But he told Jack he was to heed none of them, but press through room after room till he come to the sixth room, and there he would find the Queen herself asleep, with the little child by her side. So Jack went meeting the dhragon this third day again, and the dhragon come meeting Jack. And he opened his mouth as wide as the world, and let a roar that rattled the eyes in the sockets of the great grey eagle on top of Croaghpathrick mountain at home in Ireland, and then fell on Jack, and Jack fell on him; and he to it, and Jack to it, and both of them to it; and if the fight was wild and terrible the first two days it was ten times wilder and terribler this day. And harder and harder it was getting the more they warmed to the work; and one time it was Jack was getting the better of the dhragon, and the next time it was the dhragon was getting the better of poor Jack; and at last coming on tor'st night the dhragon was putting very hard on Jack entirely, and it was very nearly being all over with him, when he stepped back, and gathering all his strength mounted into the air with one spring, and come down atop of the dhragon's head, and struck his sword into his heart, leaving him over dead. Then Jack went into the Castle, and no sooner did he go in than there was lots of the most beautiful virgins, running in great commotion, and asking Jack, "Is it me ye want? Is it me ye want?" But Jack never heeded thim till he come into the sixth room, where he saw the beautiful Queen of the Golden Mines asleep, with the Queen of France's child asleep beside her. Jack bent over her and gave her one kiss, for she was a lovely picthur. Then he took up the child in his arms, and picking up a beautiful garter all glancing with diamonds, that was lying by the Queen's bedside, and taking with him a loaf of bread that could never be eaten out, a bottle of wine that could never be drunk out, and a purse that could never be emptied, he started away. He stopped that night with the ould man, who took down his bottle of ointment and healed up all the wounds Jack got that day. In the morning Jack started for France, leaving with the ould man to keep till the Queen of the Golden Mines would call for it the purse that never could be emptied. When Jack reached France, and presented back to the

Queen her darling child, that was the rejoicement and the joy!
There was a great faist given, and at the faist Jack said he had a
little wondher he fetched with him, that he'd like to show; and
he produced his bottle, and sent it round the prences, and nobility, and genthry that were all assembled at the faist, and axed
them all to drink the Queen's health out of it. This they all did;
and lo! and behold ye, when they had finished the bottle was as
full as when they commenced; and they all said that bate all ever
they knew or heerd tell of; and the King said it bate all ever he
knew or heerd tell of, too, and that the same bottle would be of
mighty great sarvice to him, to keep his troops in drink when
he'd go to war, and axed Jack on what tarms he'd part with it.
Jack said he couldn't part with it entirely, as it wasn't his own,
but if the King relaised his brother he'd leave the bottle with
him till such times as the Queen of the Golden Mines might call
for it. The King agreed to this. Jack's brother was relaised, and
himself and Jack started off for England. When they were come
there the King of England gave a great faist in their honour, too,
and at this faist Jack said he'd like to show them a little wonder
he fetched with him, and he produced the loaf, and axed the
King to divide all round. And the King cut off the loaf, and
divided all round, over all the prences and nobility and gentry
that was there; and when he had finished they were all lost in
wondherment, for the loaf was still as big as when the King commenced to cut. The King said that would be the grand loaf for
feeding his troops whenever he went to war, and axed Jack what
would he take to part with it. Jack said the loaf wasn't his to part
with, but if the King relaised his brother out of prison he'd give
him the loaf till such times as the Queen of the Golden Mines
might call for it. The King agreed to this, and relaised Jack's
other brother, and then the three of them started for home
together. And when they were come near home the two older
brothers agreed that Jack when he'd tell his story would disgrace
them, and they'd put him to death. But Jack agreed if they'd let
him live he would go away and push his fortune, and never go
back near home. They let him live on these conditions, and they
pushed on home, where they were received with great welcomes, and told mortial great things entirely of all the great

things they done while they were away. Jack come to the castle in disguise and got hired as a boy and lived there.

The Queen of the Golden Mines, when she woke up and learned of the young gentleman that had killed the dhragon, and carried off the child and the other things, and kissed her, said he must be a fine fellow entirely, and she would never marry another man if she couldn't find him out. She got no rest till she started, herself and her virgins, and away to find out Jack. She first come to the old man, where she got her purse, and he directed her to the King of France. When she come to the Court of the King of France she got her bottle, and he said Jack went from there to go to see the King of England. From the King of England she got her loaf, and he diracted her to Ireland, telling her that Jack was no other than the King of Ireland's son. She lost no time then reaching the Court of the King of Ireland, where she demanded his son who had killed the fiery dhragon. The King sent out his eldest son, and he said it was him that had killed the fiery dhragon, and she asked him for tokens, but he could give none, so she said he wasn't the man she wanted. Then the King's second son come out and said it was him killed the fiery dhragon. But he couldn't show her no tokens either, so he wouldn't do. Then the King said he had no other son, but a good-for-nothing *droich* who went away somewhere and never come back; but that it wasn't him anyhow, for he couldn't kill a cockroach. She said she'd have to see him, and converse with him, or otherwise she wouldn't go away till she'd pull down his castle. Then the whole house was upside down, and they didn't know what to do. And Jack, who was doing something about the yards, axed what it was all about; and they told him, and he axed to have a minute's convarsing with her. But they all laughed at him; and one gave him a knock, and another gave him a push, and another gave him a kick. And Jack never minded them one bit, but went out and said it was him that kilt the fiery dhragon. They all set up another big roar of a laugh at this. Then the Queen asked him to show his tokens, and Jack fetched from his pocket the beautiful garter, all shining with jewels, and held it up, and the Queen came and threw her arms about Jack's neck and kissed him, and said he was the brave man she'd marry, and no other. And my brave Jack, to the astonishment of them all, confessed who he was, and got married to her, and was ever afther the King of the Golden Mines.

# The Widow's Daughter

THERE WAS ONCE a poor widow woman, living in the North of Ireland, who had one daughter named Nabla. And Nabla grew up both idle and lazy, till at length, when she had grown to be a young woman, she was both thriftless and useless, fit only to sit with her heels in the ashes and croon to the cat the day long. Her mother was annoyed with her, so that one day, when Nabla refused to do some little trifle about the house, her mother got out a good stout sallyrod and came in and thrashed her soundly with it.

As her mother was giving Nabla the whacking she had so richly earned, who should happen to be riding past but the King's son himself. He heard the mother walloping and scolding, and Nabla crying and pleading within. So he drew rein, and at the top of his voice shouted to know what was the matter. The widow came to the door, curtseying when she saw who he was. Not wishing to give out a bad name on her daughter, she told the King's son that she had a daughter who killed herself working the leelong day and refused to rest when her mother asked her, so that she had always to be beaten before she would stop.

"What work can your daughter do?" the Prince asked.

"She can spin, weave and sew, and do every work that ever a woman did," the mother replied.

Now, it so happened that a twelvemonth before the Prince had taken a notion of marrying, and his mother, anxious he should have none but the best wife, had, with his approval, sent messengers over all Ireland to find him a woman who could perform all a woman's duties, including the three accomplishments the widow named—spinning, that is, weaving and sewing. But all the candidates whom the messengers had secured were found unsatisfactory on being put to trial, and the Prince had remained unwedded. When, now, the King's son heard this account of Nabla from her own mother, he said:

"You are not fit to have the charge of such a good girl. For twelve months, through all parts of my mother's kingdom, search was being made for just such a young woman that she might become my wife. I'll take Nabla with me."

Poor Nabla was rejoiced and her mother astonished. The King's son helped Nabla to a seat behind him on the horse's back and bidding adieu to the widow rode off.

When he had got Nabla home, he introduced her to his mother, telling the Queen that by good fortune he had secured the very woman they had so long sought in vain. The Queen asked what Nabla could do, and he replied that she could spin, weave and sew, and do everything else a woman should; and, moreover, she was so eager for work that her mother was flailing her within an inch of her life to make her rest herself when he arrived on the scene at Nabla's own cottage. The Queen said that was well.

She took Nabla to a large room and gave her a heap of silk and a golden wheel, and told her she must have all the silk spun into thread in twenty-four hours. Then she bolted her in.

Poor Nabla, in amazement, sat looking at the big heap of silk and the golden wheel. And at length she began to cry, for she had not spun a yard of thread in all her life. As she cried an ugly woman, having one of her feet as big as a bolster, appeared before her.

"What are you crying for?" she asked.

Nabla told her, and the woman said, "I'll spin the silk for you if you ask me to the wedding."

"I'll do that," Nabla said. And then the woman sat down to the wheel, and working it with her big foot, very soon had the whole heap spun.

When the Queen came and found all spun she said: "That is good." Then she brought in a golden loom and told Nabla she must have all that thread woven in twenty-four hours.

When the Queen had gone Nabla sat down and looked from the thread to the loom and from the loom to the thread, wondering, for she had not in all her life even thrown a shuttle. At length she put her face in her hands and began to cry. There now appeared to her an ugly woman with one hand as big as a pot hanging by her side. She asked Nabla why she cried. Nabla told her, and then the woman said:

"I'll weave all that for you if you'll give me the promise of your wedding."

Nabla said she would surely. So the woman sat down to the golden loom, and very soon had all the thread woven into webs.

When again the Queen came and found all woven she said: "That is good." And then she gave Nabla a golden needle and thimble and said that in twenty-four hours more she must have all the webs made into shirts for the Prince.

Again when the Queen had gone, Nabla, who had never even threaded a needle in all her life, sat for a while looking at the needle and thimble and looking at the webs of silk. And again she broke down, and began to cry heartily.

As she cried an ugly woman with a monstrously big nose came into the room and asked:

"Why do you cry?"

When Nabla had told her, the ugly woman said:

"I'll make up all those webs into shirts for the Prince if you promise me the wedding."

"I'll do that," Nabla said, "and a thousand welcomes."

So the woman with the big nose, taking the needle and thimble, sat down, and in a short time had made all the silk into shirts and disappeared again.

When the Queen came a third time and found all the silk made up in shirts she was mightily pleased and said:

"You are the very woman for my son, for he'll never want a housekeeper while he has you."

Then Nabla and the Prince were betrothed, and on the wedding night there was a gay and a gorgeous company in the hall of the Castle. All was mirth and festivity. But as they were about to sit down to a splendid repast there was a loud knock at the door. A servant opened it and there came in an ugly old woman with one foot as big as a pot who, amid the loud laughter of the company, hobbled up the floor and took a seat at the table. She was asked of which party was she, the bride or the groom's, and she replied that she was of the bride's party. When the Prince heard this he believed that she was one of Nabla's poor friends. He went up to her and asked her what had made her foot so big. "Spinning," she said, "I have been all my life at the wheel, and that's what it has done for me." "Then, by my word," said the Prince, striking the table a great blow, "my wife shall not turn a wheel while I'm here to prevent it!"

As the party were again settling themselves another knock came to the door. A servant opening it, let in a woman with one hand as big as a stool. The weight of this hand hanging by her side gave her body a great lean over, so that as she hobbled up the floor the company at the table lay back, laughing and clapping their hands at the funny sight. This woman, taking a seat at the table, was asked by whose invitation she was there, to which she replied that she was of the bride's party. Then the Prince went up to her and inquired what caused her hand to be so big.

"Weaving," she said. "I have slaved at the shuttle all my life; that's what has come on me."

"Then," the Prince said, striking the table a thundering blow, "by my word, my wife shall never throw a shuttle again while I live to prevent it."

A third time the company were ready to begin their repast, when again there came a knock to the door. Every one looked up; and they saw the servant now admit an ugly old woman with the most monstrous nose ever beheld. This woman likewise took a chair at the table. She was then asked who had invited her, the bride or the groom. She said she was one of the bride's party. Then the Prince, going up to her, asked her why her nose had come to be so very big.

"It's with sewing," she said. "All my life I have been bending my head over sewing, so that every drop of blood ran down into my nose, swelling it out like that."

Then the Prince struck the table a blow that made the dishes leap and rattle.

"By my word," he said, "my wife shall never either put a

needle in cloth again or do any other sort of household work while I live to prevent it."

And the Prince faithfully kept his word. He was always on the lookout to try and catch Nabla spinning, weaving or sewing, or doing any other sort of work, for he thought she might at any time try to work on the sly.

Poor Nabla, however, never did anything to confirm his uneasiness, but, taking her old mother to stop in the Castle with her, lived happy and contented, and as lazy as the day was long, ever after.

# Shan Ban and Ned Flynn

SHAN BAN and Ned Flynn were neighbouring farmers that wrought hard on their wee bits of farms to support themselves and their wives—but that same was more nor they could do; so says Shan Ban to Ned Flynn one day, "Ned," says he, "what do ye think if we start off to push our fortunes, and leave our wives to look out for themselves for a while?" "Why, I think," says Ned, says he, "it wouldn't be a bad idea at all." No sooner sayed than done, off both of them starts, and away afore them to push their fortunes. They thravelled away for the length of a day, without meeting with anything remarkable, and long afther night fell on them they were still wanderin' on when Shan sees a light away from him, and "Ned," says he, "I think we'll dhraw on that light." Well and good, on the light they dhrew, and when they come there, they found the light was shining from a great castle, and in they went to the castle, and finding or seeing no one there, they wandhered on through it from room to room, dumfoundered with all the gorgeous grandeur, goold an' silver, they saw everywhere. At last they come to a great dining-room, with a great dinner entirely, of all sorts of the richest and grandest, and nicest eating and drinking spread out on the tables. "Come, help ourselves," says Shan, "we'll line our insides anyhow." "A good job," says Ned; and both of them fell to, and made a hearty meal. Then all at once they heard music and the tramping of feet coming tor'st them. "We'll have to hide," says Shan; and "I think it's best," says Ned. So both of them took and hid themselves under a sofa where they couldn't be seen. Ned wasn't right under the sofa when he was fast asleep by reason of the big dinner he ate. But Shan kept wide awake, and peeping out through a little hole in the sofa cloth could see all that was going on. Into the room came a company of five hundred fairies, little men and women, all grandly dressed in every colour of silks and satins and ribbons, with forty little pipers playing before them, and they dancing along behind with their hands caught. When they come in, the forty pipers played three times round the dinner table till the rest of the company bowed to one another and got saited, and then the pipers laid aside their pipes and sat down themselves. Afther they had made a good dinner, the decanthers of all sorts of whiskies and wines and rare drinks was put on the table, and then the little man that sat at the head give it out that every one present would have to sing a song, crack a joke, or tell a good tale. And round the table at once went the singing and the joking and the telling of the stories. Says one of the fairies, "I'll tell a good story"; and he begun to tell how the King's daughter was lying very ill, and all the great doctors of the country was attending to her; but it was all no use, for she was pining away day afther day under the fairies' spells, and there was nothing in the world could save her except three mouthfuls of the dandylion which grew on the Grey Forth, and which had the virtue of curing all diseases. Shan Ban's heart jumped when he heard this, and he waited patiently till, when day was going to break, the pipers got up and took their pipes, and the company got up, and the pipers played afore them out of the room, and the fairies danced out afther. Then Shan wakened up Ned, and taking him with him went out and up the Grey Forth, plucked the dandylion that grew there, never letting on to Ned what he meant by it, and both of them started away for the King's palace. When they were come there they knocked, and the sarvints axed them what they wanted, and Shan said he had come to try and cure the King's daughter. The sarvints of course only laughed at Shan, but the King hearing of him ordered him to be brought up. And when Shan was brought up into the princess's bed-chamber there that place was filled with great doctors, and when they heard Shan was coming to try to cure the princess they laughed hearty. But the King said they had their try and made nothing of it, and that Shan Ban might as well get his try, for he couldn't have worse luck nor them any-how. Then Shan ordered all the doctors out of the room, and giving the princess one mouthful of the dandylion she got great aise entirely, then he gave her another mouthful, and she felt a deal better still; then he gave her the third mouthful, and she was completely cured. There was great rejoicement entirely at this, and the King in particular was beside himself with delight and offered Shan Ban the princess in marriage. But Shan wouldn't have her on no account, for he said he wouldn't part his wife Molly at home for all the princesses in the world, no mat-ter how beautiful they might be. Then the King filled two bags, one with goold and the other with silver, and give them to Shan. When Shan got outside the castle he handed the two bags to Ned and told him to take them home with him, and give his (Shan's) wife the bag of goold and keep the bag of silver for him-self; and that he wouldn't go home himself till he would thravel further and see were there any more adventures. Then both of them parted, Ned for home with the bags of money and Shan travelling away further before him. Shan travelled on that day till at night falling he was getting into a wood, when what does he see sitting on a sycamore leaf but the identical same little fairy that told at the supper the story about the King's daughter. "Shan Ban, Shan Ban," says the little fellow, "you hid and lis-tened to our stories the other night and heard me tell the secret of the King's daughter and the dandylion on the Grey Forth, and then ye went and cured the princess. What did ye do that for?" "Well, small blame to me," says Shan, "I had to hide, and I couldn't help hearing yer story; and sure I'd be an onnatural man, out and out, if I didn't save the poor princess's life when I had it in my power to do it so aisy. Small blame to me, I say again," says Shan. "Well, that's surely true," says the fairy, "but that's a mighty great saicret, that about the dandylion, and if it got out it's I would be blamed for it, and I would never hear the last of it nor get any living afther from the rest of the fairies, and I would be made a miserable devil entirely." "Well, if that's so," says Shan, "the saicret's a saicret yet, for man or mortal didn't hear it from me; and if it's a consolation to ye I promise ye it'll be so." "Thanky, very much," says the fairy; "it's certainly a

consolation and a great one, and I know I may depend on yer
promise. And, when you're so mighty kind, Shan Ban," says he,
"I'll be every bit as kind. Here's a napkin for ye that ye have only
to spread it out and wish for what ye like, and as much as ye like,
of aitables and drinkables, and immediately they will be placed
on it. And here's a wishing cap," says he, "ye have only to put on
yer head and wish to be any place in the world ye like, and
immediately ye'll be there. And here's a purse filled with money,
that no matther how much ye take out of it it will never get
empty." He handed over to Shan the napkin, the wishing cap,
and the purse, and then disappeared without even waiting to be
thanked. Shan was feeling just hungry enough, and he spread
out the napkin to try it. He wished for a nice supper for himself,
and, lo and behold ye! all at once there was the rarest supper,
aiting and drinking, ever he laid his two eyes on, spread on the
napkin. He ate and drunk heartily, and then spread himself out
under the trees to sleep. In the morning Shan got up and spread
his napkin and wished for a breakwus, and had the finest of aiting and drinking again, his hearty fill, and then he set off on his
journey once more. Tor'st evening he was travelling in a very
bare and barren country, without any people, or anything growing that a man could ate, or anything flowing that a man could
drink. And here, as he spread his napkin and had a beautiful dinner on it, who should come up to him, weary and worn, but a
piper: and Shan axed him to sit down and help him with dinner.
Nothing loath, down the piper sat, for he was most dead with
the hunger; and both of them ate as good a dinner as ever they
ate in their lives afore. When they were finished the piper
pulled out a horn, and commenced to play his pipes, and four
hundred thousand troopers—Light Dhragoons, Heavy
Dhragoons, Hussians, Grenadiers, and Kilties—come troopin'
out of the horn, and begun dancing to the music. Then the piper
told Shan he was under great distress entirely, because for the
last five days, being in this barren country, he hadn't a bit to put
in the mouths of his troopers, and they were dying with hunger.
Then says Shan, "I'll soon relieve them," and he spread his napkin and wished for aiting and drinking for four hundred thousand troopers, and immaidiately it was on the napkin, and the

troopers all ate and drunk to their satisfaction, and went in to
the horn again. "Well," says the piper, "that is a wondherful
great napkin entirely, and I wouldn't care if I had it instead of
my horn of troopers—for what use are they to me if I can't feed
them?" "I'll swap with ye, the napkin for the horn," says Shan.
"Done," says the piper, and handing over to Shan the horn, he
took the napkin and started off. But when my brave Shan found
himself in possession of the horn and four hundred thousand
troopers he axed himself how was he going to get them fed at
all, at all. And says he, "If I only had the napkin now to feed
them I'd be a happy man." At once he ordhered the troopers out
of the horn, and they come tumbling out—Light Dhragoons,
Heavy Dhragoons, Hussians, Grenadiers, and Kilties—and
away he sent them after the piper to take the napkin from him.
And when they brought Shan the napkin he ordered them again
into their horn, and said he'd now go for home. So he put the
wishing cap on his head and wished to be home. And when he
got there and looked about him he couldn't know it was the
same country at all, at all, for there, in the place where Ned
Flynn's house used to be, was a great castle with gardens, and
lawns, and parks all round it. He come up to the door of his own
house, and Molly was the glad woman to see him back. "And
what," says he to Molly, "is the meanin' of that great castle
where Ned Flynn's cabin used to be?" "Oh," says Molly, says
she, "sure Ned Flynn was away, no one knows where, pushing
his fortune, and he come home with no end of bags of money
with him, and had up that grand castle and all them parks and
lawns before ye'd have time to look about ye. He's now very rich
entirely, and, doesn't know his own wealth." "And Molly," says
Shan, "was he any way kind to you when he came back with so
much money, or did he make ye ever a present?" "Kind!" says
Molly; "kind's no name for it. He give me five shillings the day
afther he come home, and has ordhered me an' allowance of
half-a-crown a week ever since." Says Shan, "I must set off to see
him." "Oh, no, ahasky, Shan," says Molly, "ye couldn't go to see
him in them old clothes, or he'd ordher you to be shot." But
Shan set off to Ned Flynn's castle, and when he was come there
he inquired of the servants to see Lord Flynn. But they told him

they couldn't let him into his lordship's presence at all, at all, in such old clothes as he had on him. But Lord Flynn heard that Shan Ban was at the door wanting to get in to see him, and he ordhered the servants to let him in and bring him upstairs to him. He shook hands heartily with Shan, and said he was glad to see him home again. John thanked him, and said his wife, Molly, was telling him that he had been very good to her, and he thanked him entirely for this. Then Lord Flynn said he was going to give a great ball, and, to show he had no ill-will again' Shan, axed himself and his wife to come to it. Shan and Molly attended the ball, and then axed Lord Flynn and his wife to come to their house to a ball next night. When Shan got home, says Molly to him, says she, "Shan, do ye intend enthertaining Lord Flynn and his wife? Sure ye haven't a proper house to take them to; nor ye have no money to buy provisions to enthertain them properly." "Oh, we'll soon rightify that," says Shan. He took out the purse and covered the floor with gold, and filled up a room full of it. He then ordhered out his four hundred thousand troopers out of the horn, and set them to work building a great castle, and before the next night he had the castle up, and all its walls lined with silver, and its floors of beaten gold, and he had a gold walk right from the door of it to Lord Flynn's castle. And when Lord Flynn and his wife come they were all in wondherment and didn't know what to make of it at all. And Shan Ban and Molly welcomed them, and they dressed up in the most gorgeous dresses, and Molly with two diamonds hanging from her ears, the size of turf. Then there was no end of sarvints in waiting, and the napkin was spread, and Shan wished for the grandest supper that ever was, and immediately the grandest that ever was seen, afore or since, was before them. And when Lord Flynn got home, he sent a messenger to the King to tell him of the wondherful napkin Shan Ban had, and that it would be of great sarvice to the King in times of war, and axed the King to send his sojers for it. So the King sent thirty sojers to demand the napkin of Shan; but Shan turned out sixty sojers out of his horn who fell on the King's sojers and killed them all but one, who went home and told the King. Then the King sent ten thousand troopers; but Shan turned fifty thousand troopers out of the horn, and killed all the king's men to one, again. Then the King sent a hundred thousand troopers; and Shan now turned out of the horn his four hundred thousand troopers—Light Dhragoons, Heavy Dhragoons, Hussians, Grenadiers, and Kilties—and they fell on the King's men, and not one of them at all, at all, escaped this time. Then the King come to parley with Shan, and he made paice with him, and said it was Lord Flynn who had told him about the napkin, and put him up to taking it from Shan. So Shan once again turned out his troopers—Light Dhragoons, Heavy Dhragoons, Hussians, Grenadiers, and Kilties—and ordhered them up to Lord Flynn's to blow up his castle and not lay a trace of him or his on the earth. And this they did, and Lord Flynn and his wife were killed, and Shan Ban and Molly, spent the remainder of their days ever afther in paice and plinty.

# When Neil a-Mughan Was Tuk

WE HAD BEEN in the middle of our story-tellin', with all our seats drawn close together round Shemishin's big hearth fire. The storm of rain and sleet without gave us no bother, only made us enjoy the comfort of the big fire, and the great stories, far more keenly. But in the middle of an excitin' story of Paudeen Mor's—a fearful adventure of his in the wilds of Georgia, when he was carrying the pack there—the latch rattled, and the door burst open, and into the middle of the floor stepped a man, with a scared look on his face, and out of whose clinging clothes, streams of water were running, and pouring over the floor. The wet hair came down his brows and fell in wet tongues, and streams were running from it. His hat leaf drooped over all like a limp rag.

"God bliss all here!" he said.

"And yerself likewise," we said, when we got our breaths.

"Thank God!" said he from his heart. "It's me is the glad man to get a Christian roof over me head. I've been tuk."

"What? By the fairies? On such a night?"

"The fairies," Shemishin said, rebuking us, "wouldn't take any Christun on such a night."

"They wouldn't," said the stranger, "and didn't. I was tuk by Willie-the-Wisp."

"God help ye, poor man," Shemishin said, "ye had a narrow escape." And, "God help ye, poor man," we all said, and made room for him amongst us.

"I'm Neil a-Mughan of Tievahurkey," said he. "I was comin' from Donegal where I was in payin' the rent to Misther Martin.

37

It was mortial dark an' I feared I'd lose me way. Two mile back I seen the light in from me, an' I dhrew on it thinkin' of course it was a house. An' as I stumbled on, it seemed farther and farther away. I was gettin' deeper in the mire at every step I tuk, but I sthruggled on for the dear life to reach that light. I darsay it tuk me a long mile, among such marshes and bog-holes that only God willed it, and I had some poor body's prayer about me, I couldn't have escaped with the life. Three times runnin' I was steppin' intil a bog-hole when somethin' (I thought) toul' me not to lay down me foot—I held it back, and looked, and the black bottomless wather lay right at me toe——"

"Musha, God was by ye."

"He was. Thanks be till Him, this night——"

"Amen! Amen!"

"Well, when I'd gone the full mile, an' seen I was only gettin' more hopelesser into the bog, it sthruck me like a flash that it was no other nor Willie-the-Wisp, and all at wanst, I seen how I'd been deluded and a'most lost. But there I was in the middle of a black threacherous bog in a night as sleety and wet as sorra, and as dark as the inside of a cow, an' where the next step might mean death. I turned, as nearly as I could think, in the same direction I had come—an' yous may take my word for it that I was prayin' faster nor I was used to. If I have any idea of time that's two solid hours ago—and here I am now! This is the first sign of Christianity I've seen. How I got out of the bog is more nor I can tell meself—only I know God (praise be till Him!) was guidin' me steps."

Poor Norah, when she recovered sufficiently from the shock of both the stranger's appearance, and his story, warmed him a skillet of milk, and literally insisted on pouring it down the poor fellow's throat when it must have felt like so much molten lead. But Norah would hear of no remonstrance, and Shemishin, equally well-intentioned, stood by and held the victim.

Neil a-Mughan survived. Then Norah turned Patrick Burns's only sons Charlie and Ned out of the chimney-corner in which they squatted, and stuck Neil into it—"till the hait gets in about yer heart," she said, "and dhrives all the sleet out of yer bones." She put on what she called "a pitcher of tay" for him, then

buttered several large fadges of oaten bread, and boiled four
eggs hard, and gave all to him in the corner.

Neil felt a new man as he got around these; and by sympathy
our spirits got higher, too, and we felt in the mood to hear
Shemishin (than whom there were few better fitted to do it)
give us the story of Willie-the-Wisp, and the reason for his wan-
derings, and his evil tricks upon travellers:——

In the grand old times, long, long ago, there was wanst a
blacksmith, and his name was Willie—and he was notorious
over all Ireland for the dhrinkin' sportin' way he spent all of his
life—and it was often and often prophesied for him that he'd
never come till a good ending. He had come of good family, and
besides his thrade—which was in them days a profession for a
gentleman—his people had left to him great properties both in
houses and in lands. But all these properties Willie very soon
dhrunk and sported away—and all melted like snow in summer.
When it come to that he had only his trade, Willie had purty
hard times of it; for he didn't want to work, and he didn't care to
starve—and he found it purtikilarly hard to have no money to
sport and spend, as he was used to do. He worked as little as he
could, but he wanted as much as ever; so things went on from
bad to worse, and his chances of thrade even was laivin' him, for
no man could be sartin whether he'd oblige them or refuse them
(accordingly as the mood was on him) when they'd bring a horse
to shoe, or a plough to mend. And at long and at last wan
mornin' that he had got no breakfast, bekase he had neither
money nor means, he was standin' leanin' against his own forge
doore, with his heart in his boots, when what should come up
the road but a poor miserable lookin' old fella with a pair of broken pot-hooks in his hand, and "Good man," says he to Willie,
"would ye mind doin' a little job for me, and mendin' these pot-
hooks?" Willie was in ill-humour for workin'; but with all his
faults he had always a soft spot for the poor somewhere or other
in his heart. So when he looks at the little ragged man and his
broken pot-hooks for a minute, he says, "Step inside," an' takin'
the pieces out of the old man's hand, he blew up the fire, an'
very soon made the pot-hooks all right again. "How much for

that?" says the wee old man. But Willie was mad with him for mentionin' a charge. "Well thanky, thanky," says the wee fella, "it's little money I'd have to offer ye anyhow. But since ye are so kind-hearted I'll not laive ye without givin' ye some reward. Ax me," says he, "for any three requests ye like—barrin' money or money's worth, an' I'll give them to ye." Willie at wanst seen that he was dailin' with a fairy. "Well," says Willie, "there's a lot of lazy loungers comes about me house an' forge, an' annoy me tarribly throwin' me sledge, an' sittin' themselves down in me armchair, an' sometimes even bein' so dishonest as to pick the very money out of me purse—when there's any in it. So I wish," says Willie, "first that anywan ever takes up that sledge cannot laive it down again without I let them; and I wish anywan sits down in my armchair mayn't be able to rise from it, till I allow them; and I wish that once a piece of money goes into my purse, it can't get out again till I take it out." "Yer wishes is granted, Willie," says the wee old man, "an' I'm sorry ye didn't wish for health, happiness, and Heaven," and he went away.

Then Willie was standin' leanin' in his forge-doore again ruminatin' over it all, and feelin' far more down-hearted than afore, when all at wanst he hears the noise of hoofs, and up there rides a grand gentleman entirely mounted on a great black charger. And "Helloa, Willie," says he, "what are ye so down in the mouth about this mornin'? Ye look as lorn as a March graveyard." "Small wonder I would," says Willie, says he. "And if you had the same raison it's not such a spruce jaunty lookin' gentleman you'd be this mornin'." "I'm mortial sorry for ye, Willie," says the gentleman. "Can I help ye?" "I dar'say ye could; but I don't expect ye would," says Willie. "Don't be so sartin of that," says the gentleman—"What is it ye need?" "Money," says Willie, "an' plenty of it." "How much of it?" says the gentleman. "Och, a roomful," says Willie that way, careless. "Well, a roomfull," says the gentleman, says he, "you'll have—on wan condition." "And what is the condition?" says Willie, says he, brightenin' up. "It's this," says the gentleman, "that you'll consent to give yerself to me and come with me in seven years and a day from now." At this Willie's eye went down and caught sight of one of the gentleman's feet an' he seen it was cloven. "Phew!" says Willie, says he, "is that how the hare sits?" "It's a grand offer," says the gentleman. "Just this minute ye were plannin' how ye'd do away with yerself. It's cowl' comfort to go out of the wurrl' on a hungry belly. Here ye have the offer of a roomful of money, an' a whole year to spend and sport it. Think of all the fun ye'd get out of a roomful of money in twelvemonths and a day!" "Thrue for ye," says Willie: "it's a bargain."

Without another word then, the Devil filled with goold the biggest room in Willie's house. "And now," says he, "good-bye, and be ready for me in seven years and a day from now." "I'll be ready," says Willie.

Willie had a gay and a rollickin' time and no mistake, afther that, for the seven years and a day. He made the money spin, as it was never afore known to spin in Ireland. He come to be known all over the country as the greatest sporter and spender of the day. He kept race horses, and steeple-chase horses, carriages and coaches—and everything was thrapped out in solid goold. He built castles that had a window for every day of the year—and entertained Kings in them. And bards and chiefs were as plentiful about them as rats. The fame of the great rich blacksmith spread over the known wurrl' of them days, and great distinguished tourists and genthry of all descriptions come flockin' from all arts and parts to see him, and to receive his hospitality—bekase he kept open house for all comers, and sarvints to wait on them, and coaches and coach-horses to dhrive them.

But for all his wealth, Willie couldn't stop Time from runnin'. And at long and at last the seven years and a day's sparin's was up, an' as Willie was wan day sittin' down to a grand dinner entirely among Kings and Counts an' many larned people, and people of high degree, the door of the great dinin' hall opened, and a tall gentleman walked in. Willie looked up and at the first glint he remembered him. "Good morra, Willie," says the stranger. "I suppose you know me, and are ready for me." "Good morra and good luck," says Willie, not a thrifle mismoved—"Yis, I know you, and I'm ready for ye—as soon as I get through with dinner (it would be bad manners to laive me guests at table) an' make a set of goold shoes that I've promised the King of Prooshia there below for his horse—let me inthroduce you to the King:—

King," says Willie to the King, "this is——" "A frien'," says the Devil. "——A frien'," says Willie. An' the King an' the Devil bowed, the Devil remarkin' he hoped for the pleasure of a further acquaintance with him some day. He told Willie not to hurry, an' took his place at the table, and a right hearty dinner, and then went with Willie to the forge, to see him turn out the goold shoes. "Here," says Willie, says he when he was baitin' these out on the anvil, "make yerself useful, and help me through till I be off with ye"—handin' him a sledge. The Devil took hold of the sledge with both hands and begun baitin'; but the sarra wan of him could let it go when he wanted to, for the sledge stuck to his hands like grim daith. "Come," says Willie, says he, "old man, are ye ready for the road?" "Take away this sledge out of me hands," says the Devil. "I don't recall," says Willie, "that there's anything about that in my bargain. I'm afeerd ye'll have to stick to the sledge. Come along," says he, "I'm ready." "Och, ye scoundhril," says the Devil, says he, and he dancin' all over the place, with all Willie's guests and friends standin' by brakin' their hearts laughin' at him. "Take away this sledge," says he, at long and at last, "and I'll give ye another seven years' and a day's sparin's." So, at that Willie tuk from him the sledge, and the Devil went off in mighty anger.

It was like new life to Willie startin' the next tarm. And he went at these seven years of fun and frolic, like a man at a day's work. And if the seven years afore had been a merry seven, these seven were seven times as merry. His house never emptied, and day or night the fun and carousin' never wanst ceased in it. There come more throops and bands, and Kings and Queens with all their body-sarvints than ever went to visit Solomon in all his glory. His name and fame was sounded in the utthermost ends of the earth; and in all the wurrl' again there wasn't so great a man as Willie.

But at long and at last, again, these seven years and a day passed, too. And on the very day when they were up, just as Willie, again, was sittin' down to table in the middle of Kings and Queens, and great foreign Counts, the doore of the dinin' hall opened and in steps no other than Willie's frien'. "Good morra, Willie," says he, with an ugly smile on his face as much as to say "I'm goin' to get even with ye at last, boy-o." "Good-morra and good luck," says Willie, not the laist thrifle mismoved, seemin'ly. "Willie," says he, "I hope you're ready to come with me?" "I am," says Willie—"Butler," says Willie, "bring forrid that large chair there behind you and set it here at my right hand for this gentleman, and bring him in a large plate of the best ye can find in the pot—he's going to do us the honor of pickin' a bone with us." "Thanky, thanky," says the Devil, says he, seatin' himself, and tacklin' the dinner with a rale hearty appetite.

But lo, when all had finished their dinners, and Willie had sayed grace and stood up, the Devil he couldn't rise at all, at all, for he was stuck as fast to the chair as if he had been waxed to it. "I'm ready for the road now, old man," says Willie, "—are you?" "Oh, ye notorious villain," says the Devil, "this is a purty mane thrick to play on a man in your own house, and at your own table, moreover. Relaise me from this chair," says he. "I don't remember that there was anything about that in my bar-gain," says Willie. The Devil he wriggled and wriggled, and screwed and twisted himself, till all the gentlemen and ladies present went into stitches with the laughin'. And then, says he, "Relaise me out of this chair and I'll give ye seven years and a day more." "Done," says Willie; and he relaised him, and let him go off, black in the countenance with anger and wrath.

Willie's pile of money was by no means as big as what it used to be, but there was an odious pile of it yet. And so for the next seven years, Willie run the same rigs he had done afore; only, if anything, he went it ten times faster and furiouser, and his house was the resort for ten times as many princes and people from the very corners of the earth itself. And the fun was ten times as big, and the aitin' and dhrinkin' ten times as great and grand. And the likes of it never had been seen afore nor never will be seen again.

But the best of things must some time or other come till an end. And so it seemed with Willie; for these years passed, too. And the day the devil was due, come; and on that day, just as afore, Willie, he was sittin' down till the table to dinner, along with all his great distinguished guests, when the doore of the dinin' room opens, and in walks me brave Devil again. "Good morra, Willie," says he, with the same old vicious smile. "Good morra and good luck," says Willie, as little as ever mismoved, "won't ye sit down and have a pick of dinner with us?" "Not me," says the Devil. "You fooled me twicet, but ye'll never have it to say that ye fooled me the third time. Come along," says he. "That's mighty curt," says Willie. "It's your desarts," says the Devil. "Lay down the knife and fork now, and throt." And Willie had there and then to say good-bye to his guests, an' beg their pardon for this hasty departure, an' walk off, hungry as he was, with the Devil.

It was in the heat of summer, and the roads was dhry and dusty, and the sun burnin' down on top of the two thravellers. After they'd been some hours walkin' Willie complained he was mighty thirsty. "Well," says the Devil, says he, "the first inn we come till, I'll let ye go in and have a dhrink." Says Willie, "But I haven't got a stiver on me, me purse is as emp'y as Micky Meehan's male-chist." "Neither have I a stiver," says the Devil. "What'll ye do?" "Why, as for that," says Willie, "You're such a nice obligin' fella that I know ye'll oblige me in this. All you've got to do is to turn yourself until a goold piece in my purse whilst I buy a thrait with ye." "I'll do that, with a heart and a half," says the Devil. And the first inn they come up till, the Devil thransformed himself intil a goold piece in Willie's purse, and Willie closed the purse on him. Then straight back home with him Willie marched and into his forge. He laid the purse down on the anvil, and gettin' two other sthrong lumps of fellas along with himself, he put sledges in their hands, and told them fire away and not spare themselves. So, as heavy and fast as the three of them could, they rained the blows down upon the purse on the anvil; and every blow come down, the Devil he yelled. And they struck away, and he yelled away; and he cried out and begged of Willie to let him out, and he'd give him more sparin's. And when Willie got all the fun himself and his friends needed for wan day, out of him, Willie released him from the purse, on his promisin' to give him seven years and a day more.

But poor Willie's money, which had been goin' all this time like corn in a sieve, was now run purty low. For six of the seven

years he had as gay a time and as merry as ever afore—but the
money run out with the sixth year, and poor Willie had no means
of makin' more—for he'd sooner starve than work. His friends
disappeared, too, with the money; and him that thought he
could count friends be the thousand couldn't find as much as
one single one, now, on lookin' round him. The seventh year,
then, was a purty hard one with Willie; an' he was no ways sorry
to find the end of it comin', and with it the Devil—for he had
got heart-sick, sore, and tired of the wurrl'.

And when at the end of the seventh year and a day the Devil
come again he found Willie, with the stick in his fist waitin' him.
And Willie started along with him this time with a heart and a
half. And on ahead the both of them thrudged and thravelled for
many a weary, dhreary mile, for further nor I could tell you, and
twicet further nor you could tell me, till at long at last they
reached their journey's end, and the Devil knocked on the gates
of Hell, and had both of them admitted in.

But behold you, Willie wasn't long in here till he tired of it,
and wished he was free again. So he set about makin' himself as
bothersome as he could, and *yocked* a row with everybody in it,
till they could stand him no longer, and put in a petition to the
Devil to have him put out of here, bekase there'd never be no
more comfort whilst he'd be let remain. And the Devil himself,
too, found him so throublesome that he was only too glad to give
in, and to ax the request of Willie that he'd go quietly, and laive
them in paice. But Willie was conthrary, as always he had been,
and he now refused to go till they had to join and put him out
by main force. And when they got him out, and the gates
slammed on him, Willie kicked up a racket outside, and pegged
on the gates for all he was worth, and wouldn't go away till
they'd consent to hand him out a torch, that he might see his
way by. So the Devil, through the bars of the gate, handed out
till him the torch, and told him to begone back to the wurrl' he
come from, and spend his time ever afther in leadin' good people asthray.

Back Willie come, and from that day to this, he has continued
wandherin' afore him, over hill and dale, himself and his torch;
and it's his great delight to atthract the attention of good people

that have lost their way at night, and lead them into marshes, and bogs, and swamps, where they get stuck, and sunk, and lost.

And from that day to this, owin' to the torch or wisp he carries in his hand, he has been called Willie-the-Wisp. And on our friend Neil here to-night he had evil intentions; but, as Neil remarked, he had some poor body's prayer on him, and God reached till him a helpin' hand, and led him out of the bog.

"Thank God!" we all said fervently.
And Neil said: "Thanks be to Him!"

# The Black Bull
## of the Castle of Blood

ONCE ON A TIME, long, long ago, when good people were scarcer, and enchantments more plentiful, there was a queen who had three beautiful daughters who were renowned far and wide for their handsome looks and gentle ways, and were courted by kings and princes, and many others of high degree, but hadn't yet been won by any. One day a great prince, that no one knew, and who had never been seen in that country before, came, like the others, looking for the hand of one of these beautiful ladies. But the queen approved of him, in case he was able to succeed in winning the willing hand of either of her daughters, and though he tried his very best he couldn't win either of them; for they hadn't yet seen enough of him, and didn't know enough about him to consent, either of them, to be his for life. Then, he was too proud and too haughty to spend time in his courting, like the other great gentlemen who endeavoured to win them, and when he couldn't have his desire granted at once he would not delay, but went away from the queen's court in great wrath, saying angrily that the next time he came for them they would come with him without the asking.

It wasn't long after he went away, when one morning, the queen and her three daughters sitting by a window, chatting, and looking out on the lovely grounds, saw a great black bull tramping among, and rooting up their flower beds. They were greatly annoyed at this, and the eldest daughter jumped up and ran out, seizing a bit of stick by the way to drive the bull from the garden, but when she reached the bull and struck him with the stick, the stick stuck to the bull, and her hand stuck to the

47

stick, so that she couldn't let it go. Then the bull started away, dragging her after him and over high hills, and low hills, grey mountains, and green plains he ran, with the lady still drawn after him, very soon disappearing from view of the queen's castle, and for three days and three nights he never stopped running so, till he reached another great castle, painted the colour of blood. Here the bull changed into the shape of a man, and the frightened young princess saw that he was no other than the haughty prince they had a short time before rejected.

"Now, lady," said he, "it was my last warning, when leaving your castle, that the next time I would visit you, you would come with me without being asked. You see, my word was good, whether you will or no. I now make you mistress of my castle. If you obey me you shall want for nothing, and shall be happier than even in your mother's. But if you ever dare to disobey me, your fate will be that of many unfortunate ones who went before you, and whose blood has painted my castle the colour you see it."

The princess resigned herself to her fate, making herself as comfortable as she could that night, and in the morning the prince came to her with a great bunch of keys, which he gave into her possession, saying:

"Now, since you are to be mistress of my castle, I give you charge of all the keys of it. I go away to remain away for a day, and you can pass your time pleasantly going through the castle and seeing all the beautiful rooms in it. Only this—there," said he, pointing out a key, "is one key, and do not use it, nor enter the room it opens. If you dare to do so, you will surely suffer for your idle curiosity."

Then he went away, and the princess at her leisure went through the rooms of the castle one after another, admiring their beauty and gorgeousness, until she had seen all but the forbidden room. And when she came to it she looked long at the door, and,

"Well now," she said, "I wonder what can be in that room, or why he has forbidden me to enter it. I would like to see it; and why mightn't I just turn the key and peep in? Who can know?"

So she put the key in the door and turned it, and seeing the floor covered with some red matter she put her foot in it and found it was blood. Then she was horrified on looking round the walls to see that it was hung all round with the bodies of beautiful ladies, whom she then knew the prince must have murdered. Then she quickly closed the room again, and locked it. She went to wash the blood from her foot, but found that no matter how much she tried, though she rubbed it and scrubbed it in a running stream by the castle, that she could not get even the smallest drop of the blood washed out. But she thought she could easily hide it from her lord, and went about her business unconcerned. In the evening she took bread and a basin of milk into the garden to have supper under the trees. As she drank the milk a cat crept up to lick the drops that fell from the bowl, but the princess struck the cat with her foot.

"Miaow! Miaow!" said the cat. "If you let me drink up only what milk you let drop, I will lick half the blood off your foot."

"Get out," said she, kicking the cat again. "How would you lick it off when I wasn't able to wash it off myself."

Then a robin redbreast came hopping up, picking the crumbs she let fall, and she threw a stick at the robin.

"Toowhit! Toowhit!" said the robin, "If you let me pick up what crumbs you let fall, I'll tell how to take away one half the blood on your foot."

"Get out!" said she, throwing another stick at the robin. "When I couldn't wash it off myself, how could you tell me?"

Next day the prince returned and asked for the keys. She gave them to him.

"I hope," he said, "you did not disobey me, and open the room I forbade you?"

"No," she said, "I did not."

"Show me your feet," said he.

She tried to hide the foot that was covered with blood, but it was no use, for the prince insisted on seeing it. And when he saw the blood upon it he had her killed and hung up in the secret room.

At the queen's castle there was great grief and great trouble at the loss of the princess, and on a morning about a week after she had been carried off, the queen and her two daughters sat

by the window talking of their loss, when once more the black
bull appeared in the garden rooting up the beautiful flowers and
destroying all before him. The elder of the two daughters said
she would go out and drive him away. Her mother tried to persuade her not, but she insisted, and, catching up a rake on her
way—in order to stand further from him than her sister did—
she went into the garden and struck the bull with it. But the rake
stuck to the bull and her hand stuck to the rake, and off the bull
started over high hills, low hills, grey mountains, and green
plains, running without once stopping for three days and three
nights till she at length saw a great castle the colour of blood,
and here she stopped, and the bull turned himself into a man,
and there she beheld the very prince who had gone away from
her mother's castle in wrath not long before.

"Fair princess," said he, "you may remember that when I
quitted your mother's castle my last words were that when I
came again you would come with me without my asking you.
Haven't I kept my word?"

Then he led her into the castle and told her she would be mistress of it; and, if she so willed it, might be as happy as the day
was long, for he would permit her the enjoyment of every pleasure, and put every pleasure in her way—only, let her beware
not to disobey any of his orders else the fate of many others,
whose blood now coloured the walls of his castle, would be hers.

Next morning he called her, and telling her he was going to
be absent for two days, gave her the keys of all the rooms in the
castle, telling her she might amuse herself looking through
them, and beholding their magnificence, till he returned. But
he pointed out one and warned her on her peril not to open the
room of which that was the key.

The prince departed, and the young princess immediately set
about going through the many magnificent rooms which the castle contained, and her amazement at their grandeur was great.
She had opened and entered every room but the forbidden one,
and coming to that door and examining it she began debating
with herself why it was he had ordered her noto to enter it, and
came to the conclusion that it must contain some wonderful
secret when he was so strict in excluding her from it. At length

she resolved to just open it and peep in, saying that it would be impossible for the prince ever to find out her disobedience. So she turned the key in the door, and, opening it, she saw something red on the floor, to which she put her foot and found it was blood. Then, looking round the room, she saw the horrible sight of many bodies of beautiful ladies, and her own lost sister amongst them, hung by the walls. She quickly closed the door and locked it. But she found her foot was covered with blood, and when she went to the stream that flowed by the castle to wash it, though she rubbed and rubbed ever so hard, she could not get any of the blood off her foot. Then she gave it up, saying to herself that she would manage to conceal it from her lord.

That evening as she sat under the trees in the garden eating bread and drinking milk for supper, a cat crept up to lick some drops of milk that had fallen on the ground. She kicked away the cat.

"Miaow! Miaow!" said the cat, "if you let me take what milk drops from your bowl, I shall lick one-half the blood off your foot."

"Get out!" said she, making another kick at the cat, "When I couldn't wash it off myself, I'm very sure you couldn't lick it off."

Then a robin redbreast hopped up to pick the crumbs she let fall; but she threw a stick at the robin and hunted it away.

"Toowhit! toowhit!" said the robin from the tree where it alighted. "If you let me pick up what crumbs fall from you I'll tell you how you may take one-half the blood off your foot."

"Get out!" said she, throwing another stick at him. "When I couldn't wash it off myself I'm very sure you couldn't tell me how."

At the end of the two days the prince returned and demanded the keys.

"I trust you haven't gone into the room I forbade you of?" he said. "Show me your feet."

She tried to hide the bloody foot from him, but it was of no use, for he insisted on seeing it; and, finding the blood upon it, he knew she had been in the secret room, and he immediately killed her and hung up her body beside her sister's.

About a week after the second sister's disappearance, the

queen and her only daughter, the youngest, sat in great grief by the window on a morning, trying to console each other for their great loss, when once more the black bull appeared in the garden, rooting up their flowers as before. The young princess said she would go out and drive him off. Her mother endeavoured to persuade her not to attempt it, but she insisted, and seizing a very long pole—in order to keep further from him than her elder sisters—as she went she rushed into the garden, and struck the bull with it. But the pole stuck to the bull, and her hand stuck to the pole; and the bull went off, and she went off, over high hills, low hills, grey mountains, and green plains, running on and on, without once stopping, for three days and three nights, till at length she saw a great red castle, painted all over with blood. Here the bull stopped, and changed his shape into that of a man—the very prince to whom she and her sisters had some time before refused their hands in marriage.

"Now, fair young princess," said he, "when you refused me and I quitted your mother's castle, I said that the next time I went for you, you might come without asking. Has not my word been kept?"

Then he told her that he would make her the mistress of that great castle, and that she would want for nothing to make her happiness perfect. Only, he told her, she would have to obey him in all things; otherwise, the fate of those whose blood had painted his castle would also be hers.

On the next morning the prince told her he was going away, to remain for three days, and he gave her a great bunch of keys which opened every room in the castle, and told her whilst he would be absent to amuse herself as best she could going through them, seeing their richness and beauty. But he showed her one key, and told her on no account to dare enter or open the room of which that was the key.

The prince bade her good-bye and departed, and the princess, taking the great bunch of keys, went through the castle, gazing at the beauty of the many rooms in amazement and wonder, until she had seen them all but the one he had ordered her not to open. She stood a long time before the door of this room, wondering why it was he had forbidden her to enter it and what secret could it contain that he was so anxious to keep from her. At length she resolved to open it and peep in anyhow, for how should he know whether she had disobeyed him or not. So she opened the door, and seeing the floor covered with something red, she put her foot to it to find what it was, and discovered it was blood. Then she saw a very great number of bodies of beautiful ladies who had been murdered, and hung by their long hair from hooks round the walls. Horrified by this, she hastily closed the door, and locked it. But she found her foot was covered with blood, and she went at once to the stream that flowed by the castle for the purpose of washing it. Yet, though she washed and washed, and scrubbed and rubbed for hours together, she was unable to take a single trace of blood off the foot. Then she left, saying to herself that she would be able to conceal it from the prince anyhow.

In the evening, as she ate her bread and drank her milk for supper, under the trees in the garden, a cat came creeping up to lick the drops of milk that fell from the basin.

"Oh, poor puss!" said she, "you're thirsty and that's not much milk for you. Here," said she, giving the half-finished basin to the creature—"here is a drop for you, for you're thirstier than me, and I can easily do without it."

When the cat had finished the milk, "Miaow! Miaow!" it said, "put out your foot, fair lady, till I lick half the blood off it."

"There it is, good cat," said she, putting it out, "but when I couldn't wash it off myself, I fear you won't be able."

But in a few moments the cat licked off half the blood. She thanked it very much and it went away, leaving her eating her bread.

Soon the robin redbreast came hopping up to pick the crumbs that fell from her.

"Poor robin," she said, "you are hungry and more in need of this bread than me, for I can easily do without it," and she laid down her bread till the robin had pecked to satisfaction of it.

"Toowhit! toowhit!" said the robin, then—"I can tell you, kind lady, how to take the other half of the blood off your foot, if you do it."

"Very well, then, good robin," she said, "I'll try. But when I wasn't able to wash it off myself, I fear you won't be able to help me."

"Pluck ten leaves of the yarrow to-night at midnight," said the robin. "Throw the tenth away and boil the other nine. Then wash your foot in the boiled juice and the blood will wash off."

She thanked the little robin, who flew away, and at midnight she went into the garden and plucked ten leaves of the yarrow, throwing the tenth away, and boiling the other nine. In the juice she washed her foot, and every trace of the blood was gone.

When, at the end of the three days, the prince returned, he demanded the keys.

"I hope," said he, "you haven't disobeyed me, and opened the forbidden room. Show me your feet."

She showed him her feet which would shame snow in whiteness.

"I see you have not disobeyed me," he said, "and I am glad, for I would not like to kill so beautiful a lady. Your two sisters whom I took away, and many other beautiful ladies before that, when put to the test, disobeyed me, and I killed them and hung them up by the hair in that very room. You have not disobeyed me, and I will make you my wife, for you have nothing more to fear now that I have found you are without that curiosity which is the great blemish on most women. Here," he said, handing her a white rod, "is a wand. Go to the secret room, open it, and going in, strike the bodies of your sisters with it."

She did this, and lo! her sisters came to life once more. The prince then allowed her to bring to life in the same way all the other young ladies who had been killed and hung up in the room, and they were sent to their homes again.

The young princess found herself very much in love with the prince, for he was a most handsome man; and she now gladly agreed to become his wife. Her mother was soon made acquainted with what had happened, and her joy was great at finding her beautiful daughters still alive. She came to the marriage, as did all the other nobility; and it was allowed on all hands that a more beautiful or a happier pair had never before been united. The marriage lasted nine days and nine nights; the last day and night was as good as the first, and the first as good as the last; and the handsome prince and his beautiful princess lived happily ever after.

# The Old Hag of the Forest

ONCE ON A TIME, long long ago, when there were more kings and queens in Ireland than O'Donnell's old castle has windows, and when witches and enchantments were as plentiful as blackthorn bushes, there was a king and a queen with three sons, and to every one of these sons the queen had given a hound, a hawk and a filly. The filly could overtake anything, the hound could catch anything it pursued on dry land, and the hawk could come up with anything in the air or in the water. In the course of time, when these three lads had grown up to be fine, able, strapping young men, the oldest said one day that he would go away to push his fortune. The king and the queen were vexed at this, and wrought him high up and low down to keep him from going, but it was all no use, he wouldn't be said by them, and so, asking their blessing, he mounts the filly, and, with the hawk on his shoulder, and the hound at his heels, sets out. And he told them as he was setting out, to watch, from day to day, the water that settled in the filly's hoof-tracks outside the gate, "for," says he, "as long as that water keeps clear I'm all right; but when you see it frothing, I'm fighting a hard battle; and if ever you see it turn bloody I'm either dead or under enchantment." So himself, the hound, the hawk and the filly, they started, and off with them, and they travelled away, and away, far further than I could tell you and twice further than you could tell me, till at last one evening late he comes in sight of a great castle. When he got sight of the castle he pulls up his filly, and, looking about him, he sees a small wee house convaynient and he drew on this house, and, going in, found only one old

56

woman in it and saw that it was a neat, clean little house entirely. "God save ye, young gentleman," says the woman. "God save yerself, kindly, and thanky; and can I have lodging for the night for myself, my hound, my hawk, and my filly?" says he. "Well for yourself, you can," says the old woman, says she, "but I don't like them other animals, but sure you can house them outside," says she. Very well and good, he agreed to this. When the old woman was getting his supper for him she said she supposed he was for the big fight the morrow. He axed her, "What big fight?" "And och," says she, "is that all you know about it," commencing and telling to him how that the king's daughter of the castle beyond was to be killed by a great giant the next day unless there was a man there able to beat the giant, and to any man that would fight him and beat him the king was to give his daughter in marriage and the weight of herself three times over in goold. "Och," says he, "I'll find something better to do. I'll not go near it." So the next morning early he was up betimes and pretending he was going away to hunt; but doesn't he go instead to the king's castle, and there he saw no end of a crowd gathered together from the four winds of the world, some of them thinking to fight the giant and win the king's daughter, and more of them only come out of curiosity, just to look on. But when the giant made his appearance, and they saw the sight of him, not a man of all the warriors there, covered all over as they were in coats of iron mail from the crown of their heads to the soles of their feet—the sorra resaive the one of them, but went like that, trembling with fear, for the like of such a tar-riffic giant none of them ever saw or heerd tell of before. So, my brave king's son waited on till he saw there was none of them present would venture to fight the giant, and then out he steps himself; and the giant and him to it, and the like of their fight was never witnessed in Ireland before or since, and he gave the giant enough to do, and the giant gave him enough to do; till at last, when it was going hard with him, he gave one leap into the air, and coming down with his sword just right on the giant's neck, he cut off his head, clean off, and then when he had that done he disappeared in the crowd, and after killing some game on the hills came home and gave the old woman the game for supper. That night when the

old woman was giving him his supper she told him about the
great gentleman that had killed the giant that day, and then disappeared all of a suddint into the air. And then she said that
giant's brother was to be there the morra to fight anyone that
would fight for the king's daughter, and she told him he should
go, for it would be well worth seeing. But, "Och," says he, "I'll
find something better worth doing—I'll not go near it." So after
his supper, to bed he went, and he was up again early betimes in
the morning, and making pretend he was going to hunt, he went
off to the castle again. This day the crowd was bigger than ever,
and when the giant appeared, if the first giant was tar-riffic, this
one was twice over double as tar-riffic, and he could get no man
with the heart to venture to fight him, till at length my brave
king's son had to step out this day again and encounter him.
Well, if the fight was hard the first day, it was this day double as
hard, and the giant gave him his fill of it, and he gave the giant
his fill of it, till at long and at last when it was going hard on him
he takes one spring right up into the air and landing down with
his sword on the giant's neck he cuts the head right off from the
body and then again disappeared in the crowd, and after a
while's hunting on the hills he come home with plenty of game;
and this night, just like the night afore, when the old woman was
giving him his supper she made great wonders of telling him of
the tar-riffic fight that day again between the strange gentleman
and the giant, and how he killed the giant and then disappeared
right up into the sky before all their eyes. And then she said that
on the morra the third and last giant was to fight, and she said
this would be a wonderful day entirely, and he should surely go
to see it, and to see the wonderful gentleman that killed the
other two giants. But "Och," says he, "I'll find something better
to do—I'll not go near it, to look at him or it." And the third
morning again he went to the castle, purtending that it was to
hunt he was goin', and the third giant appeared, and him far
more tar-riffic than the first two put together. And to make a
long story short, my brave king's son and himself went at it, and
the fighting was the most odious* ever was witnessed before or

---

*Odious* is a very comprehensive word in the mouth of a Donegal shanachy. It
generally means everything inexpressible by the English language.

since, and the short and the long of it was that he sprung up at
length into the air, and coming down on the giant's neck cut off
his head, and then again disappeared in the crowd and went
home; but as he was disappearing, doesn't one of the king's men
snap the shoe off his foot; so home he had to go that night wanting one shoe. Next day, and for eight days after, the king had all
his men out scouring the country far and wide to see if they
could find the owner of the shoe; but though they flocked to the
castle in thousands not one of them would the shoe fit. And
every one of these days the king's son was out with his filly, his
hawk and his hound on the hills hunting. At last one day the old
woman went to the castle and told how she had a lodger that
come home the night the last giant was kilt with one boot wanting. And the next day the king came there himself with a car-
riage and four horses and took the king's son away to his castle,
and there when they tried on him the boot, doesn't it fit him like
as if it was made on his foot; and the king gave him his daughter, and the marriage was performed, and all the whole gentry
and nobility of all the land was invited in to a big faist. But, lo
and behould ye, on that very night when all the spree was going
on, and the fun was at its heighth in the ballroom, and all were
as busy as bees in the kitchen, what would ye have of it but at
that very ins'ant doesn't there come to the kitchen window a
hare, and puts in its head and commences licking a plate of
some particular nice dainty that was cooling inside the window,
and the cook was so enraged at one of her very best dishes being
destroyed that she got up in a passion and put off her all sorts
and said it was a nice how do ye do that, with a hairo in the
house that had killed giants, a dirty hare would be allowed to
come in and spoil her cooking. This word soon came to the
groom's ears in the ball-room, and though the king and the
queen and the bride and all the nobility and gentry tried to persuade him against it he wouldn't stop, and there was no holding
of him. He said he wouldn't sleep two nights in the one bed, or
eat two meals' meat in the one house, till he would catch that
hare and bring it back dead or alive. So mounting his filly, and
taking with him his hawk and his hound, he started off hot-foot
in pursuit. He pursued the hare all that night and all the next
day, and at evening late he drew on a little wee house he saw in

a hollow, and he went in, for he was tired, and determined to rest that night. He wasn't long in, and he was warming himself at the fire, with his hound, his hawk and his filly, when he hears a noise at the wee window of the house, and there he sees a dirty wizened old hag of a woman, trembling and shaking down to her very finger tips. "Och, och, och, it's cold, cold, cold," says she, and her teeth rattling in her head. "Why don't you come in and warm yourself?" says he. "Och, I can't, I can't," says she. "I'm afeerd of them wild animals of yours. But here," says she, pulling three long hairs out of her head, and handing them in by the window to him, "here," says she, "is three of the *borochs*° we used to have in old times, and if you tie them wild beasts of yours with them then I'll go in." So he took the three hairs and tied the hawk, the hound and the filly with them, and then the old hag came in, but she was trembling no longer, and, says she, with her eyes flashing fire, "Do you know who I am?" says she. "They call me the Old Hag of the Forest, and it was my three sons you killed to win the king's daughter, but you'll pay dearly for it now," says she. With that he drew his sword, and the hag drew another, and both of them fell to it, and I couldn't be able to describe to you the terrible fight they had entirely. But at length the Old Hag of the Forest was getting too many for him, and he had to call on the help of the hound. "Hound, hound," says he, "where are you at my command?" And at this, "Hair, hair," says the old hag, says she, "hold tight." "O," says the hound, "it's hard for me to do anything and my throat a-cutting." Then he called on the hawk. "Hawk, hawk," says he, "where are you at my command?" And, "Hair, hair," says the old hag, says she, "hold tight." "O," says the hawk, "sure it's hard for me to do anything and my throat a-cutting." And then he called on the filly. "Filly, filly," says he, "where are you at my command?" "Hair, hair," says the old hag, says she, "hold tight." "O," says the filly, "sure it's hard for me to do anything and my throat a-cutting." So the end of it all was that the hag overcome him, and then taking out of her pocket a little white rod she struck him with it,

---

°The *boroch* is the rope used in tying a cow to the stake.

and turned him into a gray rock, just outside her door, and then striking the hound, the hawk and the filly with the rod she turned them into white rocks just beside him.

Now, at home, they watched the water in the filly's hoof tracks as regular as the sun rose every day, day after day, till at last they one day saw the water in the hoof tracks frothing, and they said he was fighting a hard battle; and so he was, for that was the very day himself and the first giant had the encounter. Next day it was frothing more than ever, for that was the day he was fighting the second giant, and on the third day the water frothed right up out of the tracks, and then they knew he was fighting a desperate big battle entirely; and sure enough himself and the third giant were at it hard and fast at the same ins'ant. But at length didn't they find the water turning to blood and they thought he must be killed. So the next morning the second brother set out and he said he wouldn't sleep two nights in the one bed nor eat two meals of meat in the one house till he'd find out what happened to his brother. He took his hound, his hawk and his filly with him and he traveled on and on, far further than I could tell you, and twice further than you could tell me, till at length one evening late doesn't he come to the very wee house near a great castle where his brother had put up before him. And when he comes in the old woman that was in the house flew at him and kissed him and welcomed him back with a hundred welcomes ten times over, for he was so like his brother she was sure it was him was in it. Then she told him that they were all waiting for him anxiously at the castle, expecting him back every day, and that he should lose no time in going to them, for that the bride in particular was down-hearted entirely since he had went away, thinking that she'd never see him no more. So off he starts at once for the castle to find it all out, and it's there was the welcome and the rejoicing, and the pretty king's daughter covered him all over with kisses, and there was a great spread, and all the gentry and nobility were asked in again, but that night again, what would you have of it, but the hare comes a second time, and spoiled the cook's best dish, and drove the cook into a frightful rage, and—"It's a nice how do ye do, indeed," says the cook, says she, "that with a hairo in the house that slew three giants a hare would be allowed to come in and spoil my very choicest dish, and then go off with itself scot free," says she. And this word come to the new groom in the ballroom, and "By this, and by that," says he, "I won't stop till I go after that hare, and I'll never stop two nights or eat two meals in the one house 'till I bring back that hare dead or alive." And so, off he starts, himself, the hound, the hawk, and the filly; and all that night and the next day he purshued after the hare, and late the next evening when he was feeling tired out and not able to follow any further doesn't he see in the hollow below him a little house, and drawing on the house, he went in and was warming himself by the fire with his hound, his hawk and his filly about him when he hears a noise at the window, and there he sees an old hag quaking and shaking all over. "Och, och, och, it's cold, cold, cold," says she, trembling all over. "Why don't you come in and warm yourself?" says he. "O," says she, "I couldn't go in, for I'm afeerd of them wild animals of yours. But here," says she, pulling three long hairs out of her head, "here's three of the kind of *borochs* we used to use long ago, and tie your animals with them, and then I'll go in." So he takes the hairs and ties the hound, the hawk and the filly with them, and then the old hag came in, and she not trembling at all now, but her eyes flashing fire, and, says she, "Your brother killed my three sons, and I made him pay dearly for it, and I'll make you pay dearly," says she, "too." So with that she drew a sword, and he drew a sword, and both of them to it, and they fought long and they fought hard, but the hag was too many for him, so at length he had to call on the hound. "Hound, hound," says he, "where are you at my command?" Says the old hag, says she, "Hair, hair, hold tight!" "O," says the hound, "how could I do anything and my throat a-cutting?" Then he called on the hawk. "Hawk, hawk," says he, "where are you at my command?" "Hair, hair," says the old hag, says she, "hold tight!" "O," says the hawk, "how could I do anything and my throat a-cutting?" Then he called on his filly. "Filly, filly," says he, "where are you at my command?" "Hair, hair," says the old hag, says she, "hold tight!" "O," says the filly, says he, "how could I do anything and my throat a-cutting?" So the end of it all was again that the hag got the better of him, and, taking out a wee bit of white rod out of her pocket she struck him with it, and turned him into another gray stone outside the door, and then struck the hound, the hawk and the filly, and turned them into three white stones just beside him.

Now, at home as before, they were watching his filly's hoof tracks every day regular, and everything went well till at last one day they saw the water in them turn bloody and then they were afeerd he was kilt. Then the very next morning says the youngest son, Jack, says he, "I'll start off with my hound, my hawk and my filly, and won't sleep two nights in one bed, or eat two meals in the one house till I find what has happened to my two older brothers." So off he starts—himself, his filly, his hawk, and his hound—and he traveled and traveled away, far further than you could tell me or I could tell you, till he come in sight of the very same castle his two brothers reached before him, and drawing on the wee hut he saw near it he went in, and the old woman jumped and threw her arms about his neck, and welcomed him home with a hundred thousand welcomes, and told him it was a poor thing to go away and leave his bride the way he did, twice, and that she was in a very bad way, down-hearted entirely, thinking and ruminating what had become of him, or happened to him at all, at all. And then she hurried my brave Jack off to the castle. And, och, it's there the welcome was for him and the rejoicements, bekase he had come back again. And this time, just as before, the great faist was given, and the gentry and nobility all asked in to it, and the play was at its heighth when the word come to the ballroom once more about the unmannerly hare spoiling the cook's best dish the third time, and how the cook said it was a purty how de ye do, entirely, that such a thing would be allowed, with a hairo in the house that slew three giants. And with that, without more ado, off my brave Jack insisted on starting, and there was no holding of him, good or bad, for he said he was bound to fetch back that hare, dead or alive. So off Jack starts himself, his hawk, his hound and his filly, and Jack had a sort of notion in his eye that this same hare was nothing good, and that 'twas it led his two brothers astray, whatever had happened to them. So he traveled on, and on, and on, for that night and all the next day, and never come up with the hare, till at length, late that evening, he saw from him the same wee hut in the hollow that his brothers drew on before, and on it my brave Jack drew, too. And after he had been in the cabin some time himself, his hound, his hawk and his filly, he hears the noise at the window, and there he sees the old hag, trembling and shaking and quaking, and "Och, och, och, but it's cold, cold, cold," says she: "And why," says he, "don't you come in and warm yourself?" "Och," says she, "I'm afeerd of them wild animals of yours. But here," says she, taking out of her head three hairs, "here's three of the kind of *borochs* we used to use in old times, and tie your animals with them, and then I'll go in." Jack took from her the three hairs, and, pretending to tie the hound, the hawk and the filly with them, he threw them instead into the fire. Then the old hag came in, her eyes blazing in her head, and, drawing a sword, she rushes at Jack to have his life. And Jack drew his sword and rushed at her, and both of them to it hard and fast, and they fought long and they fought hard, till at length Jack, finding the hag putting too sore on him, called on his hound. "Hound, hound, where are you at my command?" "Hair, hair," says the old hag, says she, "hold tight!" "O," says the hair, "it's hard for me to do good and me a-burning in the fire." And then Jack called on his hawk. "Hawk, hawk," says he, "where are you at my command?" "Hair, hair," says the old hag, says she, "hold tight." "O," says the hair, "it's hard for me to do good and me a-burning in the fire." Then Jack called on his filly. "Filly, filly," says he, "where are you at my command?" "Hair, hair," says the old hag, says she, "hold tight." "O," says the hair, "it's hard for me to do good and me a-burning in the fire." So the hound, the hawk and the filly all rallied to my brave Jack's aid, and the hound got hold of the hag by the heel and wouldn't let her go all she could do; and with one fling the filly broke her leg, and the hawk picked out her two eyes, so she couldn't see what she was doing, or where she was striking. So then, she cried out, "Mercy, mercy, spare my life and I'll give you back your two brothers." "All right," says Jack, "tell me where they are, and how I'm to get them." "Do you see them two gray stones," says she, "outside the door, with three smaller white ones round each of them?" "I do," says Jack. "Well," says she, "the gray stones are your brothers, and the others are their hounds, their hawks, and their fillies; and if you take water from the well at the foot of that tree below the house, and sprinkle three drops of it on each of them stones, they'll all be disenchanted again." Jack, you may suppose, didn't lose much time doing this, and lo and behold you from the stones comes up his two brothers, every one of them with his hound, his hawk, and his filly, just the same as they were before they had been enchanted by the Old Hag of the Forest, and that was the meeting and the greeting between Jack and his lost brothers, that he thought he'd never see again! But off they soon started, all of them, with their hounds, their hawks and their fillies, away back for the castle again, and the eldest brother got his bride and the faist was spread this time again and all the gentry and nobility of both that and the surrounding countries all come to attend it and do honor to the bride and groom; and such a time for eating, drinking, dancing, singing, fun and amusement was never seen before or after. Jack and the second brother started away off afterwards for home with their hounds, their hawks and their fillies with them and as much goold as they could carry. I got brogues of *brochan** and slippers of bread, a piece of a pie for telling a lie, and then come slithering home on my head.

---

*Porridge.

# Rory the Robber

Rory was the greatest robber in that whole country, and there was a great gentleman lived there who owned a great estate in a distant part of the country. But he never got any good of the estate, for whoever he sent to lift the rents was always sure to be robbed by Rory in the mountains coming home again, and maybe killed into the bargain. So the gentleman found it was no use trying to lift the rents, and for the past five years he gave up lifting them altogether. Then there was a boy named Billy come to the gentleman looking to be hired, and the gentleman axed what he could do; and Billy said he could do anything, and then the gentleman engaged him. And when that time of year came, says Billy, says he, to his masther, "Masther," says he, "are ye sendin' no one to lift your rents this year?" "No, Billy," says the masther, "for it is no use. Rory would only rob them, and maybe murder them into the bargain on the way back." Says Billy, says he, "I'll try." Well and good the masther consinted, and told Billy to harness the best horse in the stable, so that he might have a chance of escaping from Rory. "No," says Billy, "but give me the very worst horse." And the worst horse Billy saddled, and went off. And when he was going through the mountains he enquired for Rory, and finding him out, he told him, says he, "I'm Billy, the masther's boy, and I'm going to such a place" (mentioning the name of where the estate was), says he, "to collect his rents; and if you're here when I'm coming back, I'll hand the money over to you." Rory thanked him for nothing, and said he would be there right enough to take the rents from him. So, when Billy got to the estate and collected the rents in

66

gold and notes, he had it all sewed into the lining of his coat, all
except ten pounds that he changed into coppers and tied up in
a bag, and put on the saddle before him. And when he reached
the mountains on his way back, there he met Rory waiting for
him. Then, says Billy, "I want to purtend to my masther that I
made a hard fight before I gev up the money, so do you," says
he, holding out his coat, "shoot your pistols through that coat,
that I can be able to show him the marks." Then Rory shot all
his pistols through Billy's coat, making a number of holes in it.
Then Billy threw the bag of coppers on the road, and says he,
"There's the rints," and when Rory got down off his horse to lift
the bag, Billy jumped up on it, and away off, and it was one of
the swiftest horses in the country, so that Rory couldn't overtake
him, and he couldn't fire after him, because Billy was so cute as
to make him empty all his pistols into his coat.

When Billy got home to his masther, and gev him up the rints,
and told him the whole story of how he had tricked Rory, his
masther was proud of him, and couldn't make too much of him.
"But then," says the master, "it was a bad thing to take his horse,
for he'll never rest contented now till he's revenged on me."
They agreed it was best to leave back the horse with Rory, and
so Billy started, and when he fell in with the robber and gev him
up his horse, Rory said he was a clever fellow and no mistake,
and he would like Billy would join his band. Billy said well and
good, he would. Off they went, then, to the cave in the mountains where the robbers had their den, and when they came
there Rory introduced Billy to his brother robbers, and they
proposed to welcome him with a big supper. So one of their
cleverest hands was sent away to steal a sheep that they might
make a fine roast. He was a long time away and they begun to
chat about what was keeping him. "I'll bet you fifty pounds,"
says Billy to Rory, "that I steal the sheep from him." "Done,"
says Rory. Then Billy started away, and taking off a pair of splendid big top boots he had on him, he dropped one of them about
a mile from the cave in the path the robber would take coming
home with the sheep, and then travelling on about half a mile
further he dropped the other, after rubbing it well with soft mud
to make it right dirty. Then, when, not long afther, the robber

comes along with the sheep, and comes up to this boot, he looks
at it and says "It's a fine top-boot, but, bad luck to it," says he,
"it's too dirty entirely to carry, and where's the use of it anyhow
when I haven't its fellow?" On he went then himself and the
sheep till he come to the next boot, and when he seen it "Bad
scran to me," says he, "but there is its fellow, and I was unlucky
I didn't take it." So he took and tied the sheep to a stump of a
bush that was bye, and started away back to get the other top-
boot. In the meantime Billy loosed the sheep and took it to the
cave, and got his bet from Rory. Soon the robber come then to
the cave with the pair of top-boots in his hand, and told how he
tied the sheep to the stump of a bush till he'd go back and look
for the other top-boot, and how, when he come back, the sheep
was broke away, and he couldn't get her. Then Rory ordered him
to go back and steal another sheep; "And now," says he to Billy,
when he was gone, "I'll hold ye a hundred pound ye don't steal
this sheep from him." "Done," says Billy, and started off after
him. When Billy got to the place he had stole the first sheep he
hid close by, and waited till the robber come up with the next;
and when he come up Billy commenced bleatin' like a sheep
and "Bad luck be off me," says the robber, says he, "but there's
the sheep I lost." And with that he tied the sheep he had
with him now to the very same tree stump, and went over the
ditches looking for the other sheep. Billy stole round, and loosed
the sheep, and away to the cave with it, and won that hundred
pounds too.

Rory had to confess that Billy was by far the cleverest thief he
ever met, and even cleverer than himself. "I'll tell you what,"
says he to Billy, "there's one thing I want stolen, and I have been
after it for the last five years and couldn't succeed—but maybe
you'd come better speed than me; it's the King of Connaught's
black mare, the grandest and swiftest in the world, that never
was beaten yet, or never will be beaten; if I only had her, I
would defy the whole country, for none could catch me. I'll give
you, Billy," says he, "four hundred pounds in goold if ye can succeed in stealing her for me. But it's a very difficult job," says he,
"for there's always a guard of soldiers on the stable, and a man
sitting on the back of the black mare, night and day, for fear of

me stealing her." "Well," says Billy, "if I had only a good harper
to come with me I'd steal her." "Well," says Rory, "you have that
here, for I'm reckoned a first-class player on the harp, and my
father before me was harper to the Chieftain of Knockree." Well
and good, then, Billy made him disguise as a blind harper, and
they both of them set off, and the harp with them, for the King
of Connaught's castle, and Billy put Rory to play the harp before
the castle windows where there was a lot of high-up folk being
entertained. And when the King of Connaught saw the blind
harper he made him be brought in to amuse the company, and
then, of course, a dance was started, and every one was taken up
with the fun, the captain of the guards along with every one else.
Then, when Billy found the spree at its height, he went and got
a jar of whiskey and drugged it with sleeping drops, and then
went into the courtyard and lay down close by the stables, like a
drunken man fallen asleep, with the drugged jar beside him.
The guards soon saw the jar, and smelled it, and saying to themselves that there was no watch over them this night, when everybody was too taken on with the fun, and that it would be no
harm to taste just a little of it, they passed the jar round, and
every man of them fell fast asleep; and the man that was on the
horse's back dropped off it, asleep with the drink, too; and Billy
got up and went into the stable, and taking out the black mare,
started off with her to the mountains. And when Rory arrived he
was a proud man to find the King of Connaught's black mare
there before him. He counted down to Billy four hundred yel-
low, shining sovereigns, and Billy went home with his five hundred and fifty pounds, and lived an honest and happy man ever
after.

# Myles McGarry and Donal McGarry

ONCE ON A TIME there was two brothers, Myles McGarry and Donal McGarry, and they had only a *weeshy* wee bit of a sod of land that they called a farm, but it was that small that a daicent crow with any self-respect would be ashamed to live on it; and, though Myles and Donal was two hard workin', industhrus boys close on to forty-five years of age, and worked early and late, in fair weather and foul, the dickens a bit of them could make as much out of the wee sparrow park as would keep body and sowl together, so sez Myles to Donal, sez he, one mornin' in the latther end o' harwust, sez he: "Now, Donal, asthore, as we've got in the wee crop safe and sound, and there's nothing more to do again' the winther, it wouldn't hould me," sez Myles, sez he, "to sthart away and hire till the Wareday comes round again, when I'll maybe find something to do helping you to put in a wee bit of crop. In the manetime, keep you a tight grip on the farm and don't let it blow away when the wind rises." So, spitting on his staff, and wishing Donal "God prosper him," off he stharted, and away he travelled afore him for long an' long, till at length he come into a strange country, where he fell in with a gentleman-looking man; and this lad asked him where was he going, or what was a trouble to him.

"I'm looking for a masther," sez Myles.

"Well, by the powdhers," sez the gentleman-looking man, sez he, "but I'm looking for a sarvant."

"Well and good," sez Myles, sez he, "I think we could do worse nor strike up. What's your tarms?" sez Myles.

"Well, my tarms," sez the gentleman-looking man, "my tarms," sez he, "is a wee bit out of the ornery. The pay," sez he, "is purty good; I'll give fifty pounds for a good sarvant, from now till the cuckoo has called three times—only this: any boy hires with me must never confess himself out of timper, or displaised with me; at the same time that I'll agree never to confess myself out of timper or displaised with him; and if aither of us breaks this undherstanding he's to allow his two ears to be clipped off with the woolshears by the other. Do you consint to them tarms?" sez he.

"Well," sez Myles, sez he, "the tarms is what I call a bit quare; but, stillandever, considhering that I favour the look of ye—and I think you're a jintleman—and as I know that I have a fairishly good timper meself, and as the wages is nate—why, I say all things considered, I'm inclined to be of opinion that I might go further and fare worse. So considher me hired."

Very good, Myles went home with his masther and had nothing to do that night, but got a good supper, and went to his bed, and in the morning when he got up the masther was with him immediately and sez:—

"Go out," sez he, "to the barn, and start thrashin' that wee grain of corn. There's not much in it," sez he, "and ye'll not get your breakwist till you have done."

Well and good. Off Myles started, whistling, to the barn. But when he got there and looked in of the door, my faix, his tune was soon changed, for there was as good as six ton of corn piled and panged up to the roof.

"Phew-ew-ew!" sez Myles, "there's some mistake here, surely. There's siveral days' thrashin' of corn there, and he can't expect one to have that done by breakwist time. But I'll do what I can, anyhow, and thrash away till they call me in."

But Myles, unfortunate Christian that he was, he thrashed and thrashed away, and if he'd been thrashin' since there wouldn't one of them have come out to call him in to his breakwist. So my poor Myles thrashed away, and pegged away, till he had a heap of corn as big as a wee hill, and a pile of straw as big as a mountain before and behind him, and by that time it was falling night, and no one having come to call him, he pitched the

flail from him as far as he could throw it and pushed for the
house. There he met the masther.

"Well, Myles," sez the masther, "it can't be that it's only now
ye're finishin' that wee grain of corn?" sez he.

"Finishin' it!" sez Myles, scornfully, that way after him—
"Finishin' it, in troth! No, nor it's not well begun. Nice thrash-
ers," sez he, "ye must have in this part of the country if they do
the like of that afore breakwist."

"Oh!" sez the masther, "so it's what ye haven't done yet, then?
Very well, ye get no breakfast till it's finished—but I won't
refuse you sleep. You can go to bed for the night, and go at it
fresh in the morning."

Myles listened to him for a while, and then he flew out in a
passion.

"And is that the way ye're goin' to thrate me, a daicent
woman's son, to send me to bed breakwistless, dinnerless, and
supperless, and go out to thrash the morra mornin' again fresh
and fastin' on the bare-footed stomach—is that the way, ye
onnatural brute, ye, is that the way——"

"Aisy, aisy," sez the masther. "Are ye angry with me, Myles?"

Then Myles minded his bargain, and he got down in the
mouth, and,

"Oh, no, no," sez he, "I'm not angry with ye at all, at all."

And with that he went to his bed, and next morning he was up
and out early to his work, and there the poor fellow worked and
sweated, and thrashed and thrashed, till he was fairly falling
down with the hunger and waikness, and he seen that at this rate
it's dead he'd be afore he got half through with the corn. And at
this time, who looks in of the barn door with a snicker of a laugh
in his throat but the masther.

"Well, Myles," sez he, "not breakwist time yet, I see?"

This was too much for flesh and blood to stand. He draws the
flail one polthogue at the lad in the door, and just barely missed
him by a hair's breadth.

"What, Myles, Myles," sez he, "sure it's not angry with me you
are?"

"Is it not, though?" sez Myles, "I wish," sez he, "the ould divel

had ye, for ye're the most onnatural brute I ever come across—
bad scran to ye!"

"All right, all right," sez he, "down on your knees with ye,"
and taking hold of the woolshears he left poor Myles' head in a
couple of minutes as bare of ears as the head of a herrin'. And
off poor Myles started for home, and reached Donal and the
farm in a woful plight. And he starts and rehearses to Donal the
whole norration of all happened to him.

"Never mind," sez Donal, sez he, when he finished—"Never
mind," sez he, "if I don't get even with him. Just you stop at
home, now, Myles," sez he, "and keep the farm from blowing
away, till I go and see how him and me can agree."

So spitting on his stick, and in the same way wishing Myles,
"God prosper him," he started off, and travelled away afore him
for days and nights till he come to the same strange country and
fell in with the very same man that Myles did. And the man said
he was looking for a good sarvant, and Donal said he was looking for a good masther; so the long and the short of it was that
Donal engaged on the very same tarms Myles did.

The very next morning after he hired, the masther tould him
to go out and thrash a wee grain of corn was in the barn afore
he'd get his breakwist. Donal went out and started the thrashing,
and the first cart he saw passin' the way going to the next town,
he gathered up a bag of the corn and threw it on it, telling the
driver to sell it in the town and fetch him back the worth of it in
provisions, aitables and so-forth. Faix, my brave Donal thrashed
away at his aise for three or four days whistlin' like a thrush, and
aitin' and drinkin' like a lord, and every day regular the ould
tyrant would come and look in, and ax him how he was getting
along. "As snug as a bug in a rug," me brave Donal would tell
him, and then whistle up a livelier jig, and the ould fella would
go away with himself, with a face as long as an undertaker's when
trade's dull, wondherin' how on earth the lad could thrash so long
without a pick of breakwist, till at last he began to get a bit mis-
doubtful of himself; and so, the fifth day, when he gleeked in,
and found Donal, if anything, in bigger heart than usual.

"Do ye hear me, my man?" sez he to Donal.

"Oh, I'm listenin'," sez Donal, going on with his whistling.

"Ye wouldn't be feeling hungry for a pick of something to eat?" sez he.

"Throgs, no; I'm thankful to you," sez Donal.

He studied on himself a while, and shook his head. "You're here now—let me see—one, two, three, four, five—this is your fifth day," sez he, "you're here, now, and what's strikin' me as odd, bite or sup didn't cross your lips since ye come here," sez he.

"Didn't they, though?" sez Donal, back again to him that way, with a knowing wink.

This give him a sort of a start. "And sure they didn't?" sez he.

"That's all you know about it, me rare ould buck," sez Donal, sez he, "I'm livin' like a prence," sez he, "on the best of everything, lavings and lashings, and no thanks to nobody," sez Donal.

"Livin' like a prence?" sez the ould fella. "An' in the name of powdher," sez he, "where did you get the mait?"

"I got it in the town," sez Donal, "where any one will get it that gives value for it. There's no day the sun rises that there doesn't pass by the barn door here, goin' to the town, a string of carts as long as the day an' the morra; an' what's aisier done nor throwin' a sack of that whait on them—an' throth," sez Donal, handlin' a couple of grains of it, "bully whait it is; the shop-keepers is sendin' me out word to send in all I can of it, and they'll insure me the top of the market—what's aisier, I say," sez Donal, sez he, "than hoistin' a sack or two of that fine whait on one of them carts betimes, an' gettin' back the worth of it in the best of everything, aitable, or drinkable?" sez Donal.

"What? my whait!" sez the curmudgeon, dancing with rage. "Is it my whait! Is it send my whait to the town, ye villainous scoundrelly——"

"Aisy, aisy, masther," sez Donal. "Aisy, avic, *are ye displaised with me?*" sez he, that way.

Ah, an' by the boots the ould fellow didn't know whether it was on his head or his heels he was, when he seen he was cornered. He changed the tune all at wanst.

"Oh, no, no," sez he, "I'm right well plaised with ye, Donal."

"I'm glad to hear it," sez Donal.

"Maybe *you're* displaised a bit with *me*," sez he to Donal, thinkin' to corner him.

"Not by no mains," sez Donal. "Ye're a bully masther, so ye are."

Well, that fared well, and the ould fellow wint away chokin' with rage, an' plottin' an' plannin, what anondher the sun he'd do to catch Donal. Me brave Donal come whistlin' home and wint to his bed, an' the nixt mornin' when he got up, his masther comes to him, and he give him two wild horses, and sends him out to plough with them, and——

"Donal," sez he pointin' out the field he was to go ploughin' in, "Donal," sez he "ye're not to leave that bit of a field till ye have it ploughed."

"Well, masther," sez Donal, sez he, "I'll do me best," and off Donal starts with the horses to the field, but, phew! if Donal was workin' at them horses from that time till now could he get them to pull in the plough. Donal soon seen that there was no use workin' with them so down he sits him on the ditch, and started up a lively lilt for company till he sees, comin' along the road, a hawker with two miserable old rickles of skin and bones that went undher the name of horses—they were broken-kneed, and broken-winded, and broken-boned and broken in everything only the appetite, and their hides was as white with stress of age as the top of Croagh Gorm on a Christmas mornin', and one of them had only three legs dhrawin' pay, and the other of them had a cough and a spit, and together they were like a walking infirm'ry, and when the hawker dhrew them up opposite where Donal was ploughin', and let them lean up again' each other to rest, sez Donal, sez he:

"Them's very manageable little bastes of yours," sez he.

"Well, sure enough, I can't complain of their being wild that way," sez the hawker.

"What do you think if you had these two fine black horses of mine?" sez Donal.

"I'd be afther not knowin' meself with pride if I had them spirited animals," sez he. "Quiet bastes like this pair of mine," sez he, "is all very well in their way; but when they come to be so very shy and backward that ye must pull them down wan hill, an' push them up the next, that's what I call," sez he, "too much of a good thing."

"Right ye are, me good man," sez Donal. "An if ye have ten poun' on ye, I'll take that of boot an' swap with ye."

"Done," sez the hawker.

An' then an' there both of them unloosed their yokes an' Donal got the ten poun', an' then tackling the two objects that it was a moral to see, into the plough, he started work at once, an' when his master comes out in the middle of the day to see how Donal was gettin' on an' seen the two morals that he was sthrivin' to drive afore him in the plough, it was hard to say whether it was his eyes or his mouth that he opened widest.

"I say, me good man," sez he.

"Say away," sez Donal, layin' on the bastes as hard as he could.

"Where's my two horses, I give ye this mornin'?"

"Make use of yer eyes," sez Donal, sez he, "an' ye'll see them."

"Get out, ye scoundhril," sez he, "them white scarecrows aren't mine. My horses were black," sez he.

"Thrue for ye, masther," sez Donal, "so they were black this morning; but they were so uncommon hard to manage that I have coloured them white since with the sweat I tuk out iv them."

"To the dickens with that for a story," sez the ould fellow, sez he, jumpin' at Donal's throat. "Get me my horses, ye ruffian ye, or be this an' be that," sez he, "I'll not leave a bone in yer body I won't make into jelly, ye morodin' thief ye!" sez he.

"What, what, masther," sez Donal, sez he, *"sure it's not angry with me ye are?"*

"Oh, no, no, not at all," sez he, comin' to his senses at wanst— "not at all," sez he, "ye're the best boy ever I had."

"An throgs, an'," sez Donal, sez he, *"you're* the best masther iver *I* had."

An' away the masther goes with his mouth in a puss, an' away goes Donal with his tongue in his cheek, an' got his breakwist, an' did as he liked the remainder of that day.

Well, there the masther was in a purty pickle, an' he didn't

know ondher the shinin' sun what to do with Donal, an' he said
to himself if he had him much longer Donal would have him
dead, desthroyed, ruinated entirely, an' robbed, so he took it
into his head that the best thing to be done was to ordher Donal
to go to the woods an' catch the wild loy-on (lion) that was killin'
an' desthroyin' all afore him, an' bring him alive to his masther's
house. "An' if that doesn't settle him," sez the masther, sez he,
to himself, "I don't know what will."

So, gettin' up betimes next mornin', he calls Donal in.

"Donal," sez he, "there's a wild loy-on in the woods beyant,
an' he's murderin' an' killin' all afore him, an' I want you go and
catch him, an' lead him up here alive afore twelve o'clock this
day, or if ye fail to do that I'll have ye beheaded as soon as ye
come back."

"All right," sez Donal, sez he, "there's no use biddin' the divil
'good-morra' 'till ye meet him, so in the meantime I'll go and
sthrive to fetch in the loy-on, an' we'll talk of the beheadin' business later."

Off for the woods then Donal starts, an' when he got there,
down on the stump of a tree me brave Donal sits, with his considherin' cap like, on him, an' "Donal, me lad," sez he to himself, "ye had a good many pulls in ye, but ye're at the en' o' yer
tether now; when yerself, me boy, an' the wild loy-on meets that
will be the last pull, an' then, och, och! the Lord be good to poor
Myles, the poor boy at home, without a lug on him," sez he,
"och, the Goodman, pity him, what's to become of him when
I'm gone?"

All at wanst Donal sees a little red man comin' forrid to him
with a bridle in his hand.

"Ye have a wee throuble on yer heart?" sez the wee red man,
sez he, when he come forrid.

"No lie for ye," sez Donal, "I have."

"I know it all," sez the wee red man, "an' cheer up, for I'll pull
ye through."

"Is it you?" sez Donal, sez he, lookin' up and down the wee
heighth of him with a comical look; for disthressed an' all as he
was, he couldn't help smilin' to himself at the consait of him. "Is
it you to pull me through?" sez Donal, sez he.

"Oh, never mind," sez the wee red man, "there's people isn't to be judged by their size," sez he, "I'm under obligations to your family," sez he, "an' I'll do you a good turn now. Take that bridle, an' when ye meet the loy-on," sez he, "shake it at him, and he'll be as meek as a mouse till ye put it on him an' lead him where ye like. But take that auger, too," sez he, "and when ye've caught the loy-on, bore a hole in the biggest tree in the wood, run the loy-on's tail through the hole an' knot it on the other side. Start him off then for the house," sez he, an' he reached the bridle an' the auger to Donal.

Donal was all dumbfoundhered seein' he'd made light of the little red man, for he now saw, sure enough, he belonged to the Good People, that no man should spake or say ill of in their hearin'. But off he starts, with the bridle an' the auger, an' a light heart, an' he soon fell in with the wild loy-on that was comin' on hot-foot, roarin' an' rampagin', to devore Donal.

"It's hungry ye are for a toothful," sez Donal, sez he, "an' maybe it's not just doin' the daicent thing to disappoint ye," sez he. "But," sez he, shakin' the bridle at him, "there's a time an' place for everythin' but cuttin' corns; an' you'll get feedin' enough if ye only hould on till I fetch ye up to my masther an' his ould mother," sez he.

An', sure enough, the vartue was in the bridle, for the minnit Donal shuk it at him the loy-on give over his rampagin', an' let Donal slip the bridle on him.

"This way, now, yer worship," sez Donal, sez he, leadin' him to the biggest tree in the wood, where he bored a hole with the auger an' knotted the loy-on's tail through it, an' then touchin' him up, started off for the house. An' the loy-on dragged up the big tree, an' ten acres of land that stuck to the roots of it, an' off to the house.

But, that was the play, when Donal come throttin' up to the house, drivin' the wild loy-on with the tree and ten acres of land to his tail, afore him, an' whistlin' like vingeance, "Whin Johnny comes marchin' home!" Och-och, but the ould boy his masther was in the devil's own quandarry, when Donal pulled up the devorin' brute and the luggage behind, right at his hall-doore, same as you might pull up an ass an' cart an'——

"Gwoh, Johnnie," sez Donal, sez he, to the loy-on.

But, me sowl! the masther didn't wait to say, "It's thankful I am," or "'Tis well ye done it," or any other little civility of the sort but slammin' out the hall-door an' barrin', boltin', an' double-lockin' it, gallops away, an' away up the stairs to the top o' the house, an' lookin' out of the garret windy.

"Hilloa, Donal," sez he.

"I'm lindin' ye my attintion as hard as I can," sez Donal.

"Clear off out o' that, ye scoundhril ye—yerself an' that brute baste. A nice article, that," sez he, "to fetch to a man's halldoore."

"Well, whither he's purty or not," sez Donal, sez he, "he's as God left him—an' that's a quistion by itself. But as for takin' him away, the bargain was, I was to fetch him here, but ye forgot to put in a coddy-stool* that I was to fetch him back; so, he's here now; an' here, with the help of the Lord, he'll remain, for, so far as I'm consarned, the sight of him at the hall-doore doesn't disturb me in the laste little bit, an' he may sit on his hunkers there till they make a guager of him, for all I care. In throgs, maybe I had my own throuble gettin' round the same buck—puttin' the comether on him first, an' the bridle afther, an' maybe, too, afther I had the bridle on him, an' all—maybe it would be a bit pleasanter job to ate one's breakwist than to fetch the same lad home," sez Donal, sez he.

"Oh, but Donal, ye know, Donal," sez the masther, "sure there'll be no livin' in the counthry at all, at all, with him, if he's goin' to make his sait there at my hall-doore," sez he.

"Well, there ye are now, masther," sez Donal, sez he, "an' there's the loy-on, an' between yerself an' him be it. Maybe," sez he, "if ye comed down an' had a *collogue* with him, ye might be able to raison him over, an' he might see his way to get up an' go off, himself and his applecart, back to the woods again," sez he, "won't ye come down, an' misure logic with him?" sez Donal.

"Well, troth, an' I'll not, Donal," sez the masther, sez he, "thry anything o' the sort. I don't fancy at all, at all, the sort of logic

---

*Donal meant "the codicil."

that's in that lad's eye. But do you, Donal avic, like the good, daicent, obligin' boy ye always were—do you take and thurn his
head right roun' and laive him back in the same place ye tuk him
from, an' I'll not aisy forget it to ye; an' moreover nor that," sez
he, "I'll niver, niver more, Donal, ax ye to do anything hard or
conthrairy again," sez he.

"Phew! not if I know it," sez Donal. "It's the dickens's own
throuble he give me to fetch him here, an' as I'm no-wise cov-
etious of honours I'll give some other man," sez he, "the privi-
lege of laiving him back."

"Donal," sez the masther, sez he, "how many poun' over an'
above yer wages will ye take, an' laive him the spot ye fetched
him from?"

"Well, masther," sez Donal, "like Terry Hanney's pig, thon
(yon) time—not puttin' the Christian in comparishment with
the pig—ye have raison with ye now. Over an' above me wages,
considherin' the mortial troublesome job I'm goin' to give
meself," sez Donal, "I'll have no objection in the world to takin'
fifty poun'," sez he, "an' laive the loy-on the spot I fetched him
from."

"Donal," sez the masther, "ye couldn't do it aisier."

"Oh, the ding a aisier I could do it," sez he. "As you think it
can be done chaiper, there he is, an' just say yer prayers, an'
square up yer wee accounts betwixt yerself an yer sowl, an' then
come down an' start in on him."

"Oh, for the sake of all the powers ever was cray-ated," sez the
masther, "don't laive go of him for yer life an' sowl. Ye'll have the
fifty pounds," sez he, "with a heart an' a half; only laive him back
where I'll nivir see a sight o' him more," sez he.

"Me jew'l, are ye," sez Donal, sez he, touchin' up the wild loy-
on, "I'll soon rid ye o' the menagerie"; an' in a jiffy he was off,
himself an' the loy-on, an' the wee farm at their tail an' me brave
Donal niver halted till he left back the loy-on at the very identical spot he caught him, an' onloosin' his tail an' takin' the bridle
off o' him, he let him go, an' the wee red man then an' there
appaired, an' Donal handed over the bridle to him, an' thanked
him from his heart, an' the both o' them parted.

Afther all this was over, the ould masther had a great consultation entirely with his ould mother as regards what they'd do with Donal, or how they were to get him away at all, at all, for the Ould Fella in the Lower Counthry could be no match for Donal; that he was a scoundhril, a rogue, an' a robber, an' that if they had him much longer they wouldn't maybe be able to call the very noses on their faces their own; an' by the time the cuckoo'd call, it's in their cowld graves they'd be when they'd hear it.

So they made up a plan that the very nixt night they'd have a regular spree an' jollification, an' invite in a wheen o' the naybours an' make Donal right hearty; and in the middle of it the ould mother would go out an' go up into the bush outside the house an' call "Cuckoo! cuckoo! cuckoo!" three times, an' when Donal would hear this—seein' he'd have the dhrop in—he wouldn't know the differ, but what it was the rale cuckoo that was callin', an' so they'd make him pack up an' go in the mornin'.

This was a gran' plan entirely; so the very nixt night they had a great spree, an' the naybours was axed in, an' "Donal," sez the masther, sez he, "we'll be makin' nowise odd o' you; ye have shown yerself a good, industhrous, obligatin' boy, that only for ye I don't know what we'd have done at all, at all," sez he, "so ye'll just dhrop in an' enjoy the night," sez he, "like any other; for we'd like to show ye whatever wee kindness we could— meself an' me poor ould mother," sez he.

Donal thanked himself an' his ould mother, an' sayed he'd surely take advantage of their very nice, kindly invitation. So Donal was at the spree, an' they put no stint of good sthrong whiskey in his way till they made him purty hearty; an' then, the masther, to show his pride in Donal—if it was thrue to him— sez:

"Donal," sez he, "could ye obligate the company by givin' us a good ould Irish song—one of the rale ould sort?" sez he.

"*Lora hainey*, I can that," sez Donal, "give them one of the rale ould style," sez he, an' he stharted up "Túirnne Mhairé," or "Mary's Wheel," with a roll that fairly put the company on their heads with delight, they niver havin' heard an Irish song afore. When he was finished, an' his masther had talked all sorts of applause to him, he commenced workin' round to prepare him for the cuckoo, the ould mother havin' gone out in the manetime to get up the bush—an' faix, a purty jinny-wran she was, an'——

"Donal," sez he, "it's wearin' round torst the time of year we'd be partin' now, an' I'm very sorry for it; for, throgs, though I didn't make no great bones about it, I had an oncommon great regard for ye, an' it's I'll be the sorry man when ye go."

"Faix then, masther," sez Donal, sez he, "I'll have the same story to tell meself. But I don't care if I engage with ye another tarm, at the same bargain," sez he.

"Oh, no, no, Donal," sez he, "that would niver do at all, at all; me mother an' me isn't just as well off in the world as we used to be, an' I think we'll have to give up keepin' a boy."

"Oh, anyhows, cheer up," sez Donal, sez he, "it's a far cry yet till the cuckoo calls. It's but young in the year, ye know."

"Oh, ay, but Donal, ye know, this is an airly saison, entirely, an' I wouldn't be at all mismoved if I'd hear the cuckoo, now, any minute. An', more by the same token," sez he, "if I wasn't very much deludhered, it was about the shape an' size of a cuckoo I obsarved back an' forrid in the bushes aback o' the house this very evenin'," sez he.

"Well, by the patch on my breeches," sez Donal, sez he, "an' that's a fairly sizeable oath, if it was a cuckoo ye saw, an' if she thries to give us any o' her lingo in this naybourhood for a good seven weeks to come yet, she'll be afther wishin' her mother was dead-born, when I have finished with her," sez he.

But, patience saize me, if the words was well out of his mouth, when "Cuckoo! Cuckoo! Cuckoo!" was called three siviral times from the bush at the end o' the house, an' the masther looked at Donal, an' Donal raiched for the loaded gun that was standin' in a corner; an' afore one o' the company could say "Do, Donal," or "Don't, Donal," he was out through the window, an' up with the gun to his shouldher, an' lets bang at the bush the cuckoo— if it was thrue for her—called from, an' down tumbles his masther's ould mother, head foremost, out of the tree, as dead as a salted herrin'.

An', och, there was then the *roolie-boolie*.

"Och, ye tarnation black-hearted rascal ye," sez the masther, sez he, "ye have done it at last, ye have done it at last! Me poor innocent ould mother!" sez he. "Och, ye murdherin' scoundhril ye, that has murdher in yer heart, murdher on yer face, an'— worse nor all—murdher on yer villainous hands!"

"Aisy, aisy, avic," sez Donal, sez he, "surely ye're not by any mains displaised with me, are ye?" sez he.

"Displaised with ye?" sez the masther, sez he, black in the face—"Is it displaised with ye? I'm not more displaised," sez he, "with the Ould Fella below, himself," sez he, "that I am with ye, ye villain ye!" sez he.

"Thank ye for that," sez Donal, sez he, dancin' with delight. "Down on yer knees," sez he, "till I get them handsome pair o' lugs off ye. You took off my poor brother Myles's lugs, an' I swore I'd be revenged on ye; so ye see I kept me oath," sez he.

So, there the ould masther had nothin' for it but go down on his two knees till Donal got the wool-shears an' clipped the two lugs bare off o' him; an' then gettin' his wages an' his fifty poun' over an' above, he tied up his kit in his red handkerchief, slung his handkerchief on the point of his stick, put his stick over his shoulder, an', whistlin' "The Girl I Left Behind Me," started to home an' to Myles; an' there he foun' Myles an' the farm just as he left them; an' he then with his money bought a naybourin' bit o' lan' that lay into his own, an' himself an' Myles lived the rest o' their lives in full an' plinty, as happy as the day was long. An' that's the end o' MYLES McGARRY AN' DONAL McGARRY.

# Nanny and Conn

ONCE ON A TIME there was a woman and her man named
Nanny and Conn, and they lived together quiet and agreeable, in peace, comfort and contentment for eighteen years,
when one day, Conn coming from the potato field to get a bit of
brakwust, he found my brave Nanny sitting in the chimney corner whillilew-ing and pillillew-ing, crying the very eyes out of
her head. When Conn came in she put her apron to her eyes
and fell to it like a man to a day's work. "Och, Conn, Conn! Conn
darling!" says she. "Why Nanny ahasky," says Conn, says he,
"what's the matter with you?" "Och, Conn, Conn, darling!" says
she, "but it's me has the sore heart this morning, thinking how
it's now eighteen years again' Patrickmas since we were made
man and wife, and yet Providence hasn't sent me a son to be a
comfort to me now in my old age! Och, Conn, Conn darling!"
says she, "but it's the sore pity of me this morning! Ochon!
Ochon!" "Well, by my boots," says Conn, says he, "but this beats
me entirely; such foolishness I never saw; and I hope," says he,
"that I'll see no more of it—for if I did, Nanny," says he, "I
couldn't live in the house with you, if you were a princess," and
with that Conn turns on his heels and away out he goes to his
work again, brakwustless, and whistling "Father Jack Walsh."
My brave Conn wrought away hard at his spade till he said to
himself it was a fair dinner time, and then, sticking the spade in
the ridge, he starts, whistling, for the house again, wondering to
himself all the time if Nanny had done crying yet for her son.
But, what would you have of it, when Conn puts his foot on the
threshel there was Nanny on one side and a neighbour woman

84

on the other; their two knees met across the fire, with no sign of
pot or pan on it, or any thing else that a hungry man would be
expecting, and the both of them—och, och, och!—keening and
ochoning, one louder nor another, that you'd think the roof
would fly off with itself away off the house, and hard to tell
which of the two of them was the worst. Conn gave a sigh and
sat down on a creepy stool in the draught of the door, with his
chin on his fists and his elbows on his knees, and he looking
wonderingly from the one to the other. At last, when he let them
get a wee bit out of breath, he found his opportunity, and says
he, that way quiet and easy like, "Ma'am," says he, "haven't ye
done with your foolish crying yet because ye didn't get a son?"
says he. "Och, no, Conn, Conn, Conn darling!" says she, "that's
not what we're crying about now at all," says she; "but—och!
och! och! ochon! Sheelah dear! Sheelah dear! Conn asthore!
Conn asthore!—it's something worse! it's something worse!"
"Well, troth," says Conn, relieved, "I'm glad to know it's worse.
What is it Nanny, ahasky?" says he. "Why, you see," says Nanny,
"och, och! ye see, it was Sheelah here, good woman, that come
into me in the morning to know what I was crying about, and
ochon! ochon! just as I was describing it to her doesn't the marly
hen come stepping in of the door there and fly up on the roost
there, and just as she gets on the roost doesn't—och! och!
ochon! Conn, Conn, machree! I can't tell it to ye! Ochon, ochon!
As the hen lit on the roost doesn't the roost—bad cess take it
this morning, and the Lord pardon me for cursing—doesn't the
roost ochone, Conn, Conn! how can I tell it to ye?—doesn't the
big roost come tumbling down, and och, Conn, ochon! if I had
a had the son I was crying for all the morning the poor child's
cradle would have been maybe in that very spot that the roost
came down on, and the poor innocent craythur asleep in it,
an'—och, Conn, Conn, darling! there the crathur would have
been killed as dead as a sthone. Och, Conn, Conn, Conn! Conn,
ochone! What's this to do at all at all? Sheelah *a mhilis!* Sheelah
*a mhilis!* what's this to do?" And there the two of them set up
the keen again, wringing their hands and rocking back and forward across the fire. Conn looked on dumbfounded for a
minute, and then jumping up off the creepy and standing in the

middle of the floor, "Well," says he, "that bangs Banagher! Such
two foolish idiots I never saw in my life! And by this and by
that," says he, "if I don't start out this minute, and I'll never dirty
a spade in the ground again, nor neither of ye will never see my
face more till after I have met three foolisher people than yous.
After I have met them I'll come home; but if I don't meet them
I'll never come back—and that's the most likely. Good-bye to
yous, and God be with yous!" So spitting on his stick, he stepped
out and travelled away before him. He travelled on, and on, and
on, till he come to a cabin, where there was the dirtiest and
wrinkledest and wizenedest old woman you ever saw, sitting on
the roadside before it, and she trying to sing a love song with a
cracked voice; but she was dressed out with ribbons that had all
the colours of the rainbow. "God save ye, ma'am," says Conn.
"God save yerself, kindly," says she; "did ye see ever a king coming along that road?" "A what?" says Conn. "A king," says the old
hag. "The king of Ireland," says she, "is now travelling over the
land to pick out the beautifullest girl he can get to be his wife,
and I'm sitting here waiting till he'll pass, not knowing but what
he'd take a notion of myself. For ye must know," says she, "that
I was told I was the most beautifullest girl in the three parish-
es." "When was that?" says Conn, "and who told it to you?" "It
was three and sixty years ago," says she, "and the lame beggar-
man told it to me." "And how long, my good woman, have you
been sitting there?" "Seven weeks, exactly, again' the morrow
night," says she. "Well, ma'am," says Conn, "I'm the king of
Ireland travelling in disguise, and I have now travelled over the
whole of my dominions, and I saw many rare beauties, every one
of them nicer than the other, but I never saw them I'd put
before yerself. It fails me to describe," says he, "the beauty of
them silver locks of yours, and them lovely eyes, and your figure
and face is beyond compare; the like of your grace I never saw
except in a born queen, while as for your complexion, it's like
couldn't be found in Ireland again," and there he was telling no
lie sure enough. The old hag was all overcome with delight over
this. She curtseyed herself down to the ground, and she then
threw her skinny arms around Conn's neck and said she was his
for evermore. "And now," says she, "wouldn't you like to have

some nice sweet kisses?" For she couldn't get at Conn's mouth, for he was striving to keep it as far away from her as he could. "Well, I don't know," says Conn. "You see the truth of it is, I've been so accustomed to kissing plain, ornery looking girls since I set on my journey—that's plain and ornery when put in comparison with your great beauty—I have been so accustomed kissing this sort of girls that I would be timorous. The sweetest of your kisses," says Conn, "might turn my head intirely, and leave me a raving man for the rest of my life." "Oh, don't be afraid of that," says she, "you know you must accustom yourself to mine anyhow, and one wee one will do ye no harm." "All right then," says Conn, "let it be a wee one." And then he held his cheek to her, and she gave him such a rousing smack as was echoed up on the hills and sent the wild goats running helter-skelter over the rocks thinking someone was shooting at them. "Now ma'am," says Conn, says he, "I'm a bit hungry, seeing meat didn't cross my mouth for the last ten hours, and I would feel obliged if you'd take me in and make me a bit of something, for fasting doesn't agree with a king." "Ah my poor dear," says she, "it's dead with the hunger you must be entirely. Come in, *a mhic,* and ye're welcome to the best my poor house can afford." So she took him in, and killed her fattest lamb, and put on a blazing big fire of fir and bog-oak, and roasted the lamb whole, and set it and a jar of whiskey before Conn. And my brave Conn ate like a man who had been fasting, not ten hours, but ten days, and he drunk like a man that hadn't drunk since he was weaned, and then he got up, and brushing down the crumbs off himself said he was going away straight back to his palace now to get on a daicent suit of clothes, and come back with a bishop and a rajimint of soldiers to marry her. She was delighted, and she wanted to kiss Conn going away, but Conn staggered with all the whiskey he had in him, and "No, no, ma'am," says he, "don't ye see that first kiss is in my head yet." So off he started, himself and his stick, and says he to himself as he went along, "Well, Nanny," says he, "there's one foolisher body in the world than you anyhow, but still I much misdoubt me if I can get another." Conn travelled on, and on, and on, till he came to a house where he found a man having his son helping him to get under a mule

and lift it up. "God save yez, and good luck to the work," says
Conn. "God save ye kindly," says the man back again to him,
"and thank ye." "Could I be of any sarvice to ye?" says Conn. "If
I can ye have only to say it." "Thank ye, kindly," says the man
back again to him, "ye can." "May I ax what do ye want to do,"
says Conn. "Why," says the man, "it's in regards of them fine
long bunches of grass ye see growing across the roof of the
house; it's a sin, sure, to see them going to loss, and I want to put
up the mule till he eats it." "And," says Conn, says he, "could ye
find no more convaynient way of letting the mule eat the grass
than that?" "I could not," says the man. "What do ye think," says
Conn, says he, "if I could point out a way that would make your
mule benefit from the grass without any trouble to you." "Well,"
says the man, says he, "I would think you would be a mighty
great genius entirely; and it would be mortal obligating to me if
you could." "What will you give me, and I will?" says Conn.
"Why," says the man, "it would be of very great use to me entirely, and save me all the trouble in the world; for, at least half a
dozen times in the year, every year, I have to do this, and I have
killed five of my sons at it already, and there's the sixth and the
last, and he'll soon go too; and I'll be dead myself next with the
weight of that mule lifting him, and holding him up till he eats
the grass. I'll give ye the mule and the slide-car," says he, "if ye
take it, and tell me an easier plan." "It's a bargain," says Conn.
And then and there he told him to go up on the house himself
and cut the grass, and carry it down, and give it to the mule. "By
the hokey," says the man, says he, "but you're right." Then Conn
took the mule and the man and his son hooked him into the
slide-car for him, and into the slide-car he got, and started off.
"Well, Nanny," says Conn to himself, as he drove along—"Well,
Nanny," says he to himself, "there's two foolisher people in the
world than you anyhow, but I misdoubt me much if I'll be able
to find a third." So he drove on, and on, and on, till he come to
a wee cabin on the roadside after night, and pulling up the mule
he went in, and found no one but an old woman in the house,
and she was so busy down on her knees blowing the fire that she
didn't see Conn coming in. So down he sat on a seat till she
would be done. "Well, musha, on ye for a fire," says she, "that ye

can't light; I must put a bit of tallow into ye." So getting up to get the tallow she sees Conn seated on the chair. "The Lord protect me," says she, frightened, "where did you come from?" "From Heaven," says Conn. "What, from Heaven?" says she— "and did you see my Manis up there?" "Yes, I did, ma'am, surely," says he. "I'll warrant ye, he's as contentious as ever?" says she. "Troth, and he is," says Conn, "there isn't a door in it he hasn't in smithereens." "See that now," says she, "looking for whiskey, I suppose?" "The very thing," says Conn; "how did ye know." "Ah, poor Manis," says she, was always fond of the wee dhrap. I suppose I will have to send him up some," says she; "Is there any allowed in?" "Oh, sartinly, sartinly," says Conn, "we must allow it in for him, or he won't leave a sound boord about the whole establishment he won't smash." "Oh, every stick and stave," says she; "that's him. I have just got a wee five gallon here," says she; "do you think you could manage it up?" "As right as the mail, ma'am," says Conn; "I have a mule and a slide-car down with me." "Oh, then, if ye have," says she, "maybe ye could fetch him some other little things, too." "With every pleasure, ma'am," says Conn. "Does Manis complain of the cold?" says she. "He's just parishing, ma'am," says Conn. "Oh, that's just Manis for ye," says she; "he was never done complaining of the cold. Don't ye think hadn't ye better take him up his overcoat?" "I think it would be no harm," says Conn. "Is he as fond of butter as ever?" says she. "He couldn't live without it, ma'am," says Conn. "Oh, that's just him—that's just Manis on the sod," says she; "ye had better take him up that little firkin." "Surely, ma'am," says Conn. "He used to be very fond of a rasher of bacon," says she. "It's the very last thing he mentioned to me not to forget," says Conn. "He's shouting," says he, "for a rasher and eggs yonder every morning he rises; but the sorra saize the like of either is to be found in that country." "Poor man," says she, "that place doesn't agree with him at all, at all. There, just take up that side of a pig with you, and here's a couple of dozen of eggs, too. I'm troubling you too much, good man," says she, "or I'd be after asking ye to take a few other wee things." "Don't mention the trouble at all, ma'am," says Conn; "I assure ye it's only a pleasure to me. As far as the mule can draw don't spare him, and after that, pile on to myself," says he. "Well, I must say," says she, stirring herself about the house and getting together a lot of wee needcessities, eatables and drinkables and clothes, "I must say," says she, "you're a mighty obliging man," and she commenced piling the things on the mule till his back was bending down with the load. "Now," says she, "I think that should keep Manis's mouth shut for a month of Sundays, anyhow. God speed ye," says she to Conn, "and thanky, and remember me to Manis." "Thank yourself, good woman," says Conn, "and the grace of God be about ye. Manis won't forget ye easy, I'll warrant ye, and he'll be surely thankful for these things— when he gets them." So off my brave Conn starts, now in the direction of his home; and he travelled on, and on, and on, whistling and singing, and eating and drinking and going on, and on, and on, till at length when he was coming near home he finds the thiraw° coming behind him, and looking back on the top of a hill he sees the old woman he met at first, and the man he took the mule from, and the last woman he met, all hurry-skurrying behind him with sticks and staves. So he saw they had found out he was tricking them, and were coming after him to take his life. Conn drew the mule and cart into a thick wood, where he hid them; and then turning his coat he commenced cutting scollops. It wasn't many minutes till the hunt was up with him. "My good man," said they, "did you see a man with a mule and cart passing this way a couple of minutes ago?" "I did," says Conn; "a daicent-looking man with a brown coat." "Oh that's him," says they, "but his looks belies him; he isn't as daicent as he is daicent-looking. So signs on it ye had nothing to do with him or ye'd have another story to tell. Tell us what way he went till we take his life." "Oh," says Conn, "yez are too late for that now, for just as he was passing by here——Do ye see that black cloud off there to the nor'aist?" "We do, we do," says they; "what about that?" "Why that same cloud," says Conn, says he, "just as he was passing by here, that very same cloud came down and carried himself, the mule and cart right away up to heaven

---

°Hubbub.

before my eyes," says Conn. "See that now," says they; and they threw down their sticks, and turned and went away home again.

Then Conn got out his mule and his load, and started afresh for home, and it's Nanny was delighted to see him, and maybe, too, it's him wasn't delighted to see Nanny, and he unpacked his load and gave Nanny as much as would feed the two of them for twelve months to come. "And now," says he, "Nanny, I'm back content and willing to live with you for the remainder of my days, for I met three such fools that you would be a wise woman compared with them—foolish and all as ye are." And Nanny and Conn lived a happy life ever afther; and Conn was never tired of telling that no matter how foolish anyone was there was far foolisher to be met in the world, and them was the truest words ever he omitted.

# The Apprentice Thief

IT WAS a lee long time ago when ould Ireland was happy and contented, with lavin's and lashin's—plenty to ait and little to do; and we had our own kings—half-a-dozen of them in every county—and our own Parlymint, and we had mines of all sorts and descriptions, both coal and copper and silver and goold—and, more betoken, the guineas was as common as tenpennies; and the farmers had fields of wheat that it was a day's journey to walk over, and the smell of them was a'most enough to satisfy a hungry man, if the like could be found in the kingdom—but that would be onpossible, barrin' on a fast day, when (the ould sinners that they were!) they used to schame it by goin' out and sniftherin' up the smell of the wheat, and fillin' themselves (the villains!) that way, till their fren's would a'most have to *sweel* some of them (the rascals) with ropes, for feared they'd bust; and the blight or the rot was nivir known on the praties, and they had tatties that big (the Cups, they called them) that I heerd me gran'father say that he heered his gran'father say that he heerd his great-gran'father (I wish him rest!) tellin' him, that in the harvest time they often scooped wan of them out, and put to *say* in it to fish for mackerel—and more betoken, the *say* in them days swarmed with every description of fish that ever put a fin in wather, and the fishermen never used hook or net, but just baled the fishes into their boats with an ould bucket. Well, howandivir, it was in them glor'us days of full and plenty that Billy Brogan lived as a sort of a cotthar to the King of Bally-shanny, and Billy had one son, Jack, that turned out to be very handy like with his fingers when he wanted anything that didn't

92

belong to him. Well, that fared well till Jack grew up to be a
stout, strappin', able lump of a *garsun*, when the king comes to
ould Billy, his father, to make complaints on Jack, seein' that he
wasn't leaving a movable thing about his castle or grounds but
he was hoising off wid him.

"Now, Billy Brogan," says the king, says he, "what is your son
Jack going to turn his hands to?"

"Why, yer, highness," says Billy, that way, back to him, "throgs,
I think he'll turn his hand to anything you laive in his way."

"Och! I know that," says the king, says he, "to my own cost;
but I mean to say it's near time you were thinkin' of givin' him a
thrade, for the short and the long of it is, that I won't have him
about my house or place, longer. I caught him," says he, "only
last night thrying to carry off the best mare I have in my stables,
Light-o'-foot, and that, you know, is high thrayson; and ye know
that the lightest punishment for high thrayson is to be burned,
beheaded, and hung. But I'll pardon him on conditions that you
put him to a thrade at wanst, and that at the end of three years
he'll be so parfect at the thrade that I can't puzzle him in any
three things I'll put afore him to do; but if there's any one of
them he can't do, he'll have to suffer his fate for high thrayson."

"Why, yer kingship," says Billy, "the tarms is mortial hard,
stillandiver we'll have to do our best, and sure the best can do
no more. But what thrade will I 'prentice him to?"

"As for that," says the king, says he, "plaise yourself, only
mind my conditions."

"Well," says Billy, says he, in a brown study that way, "I think
the only thrade that ever I could make an honest thradesman of
him at, would be a thief, for I think it's the only one he has the
inclinations for."

"Plaise yerself, Billy," says the king back to him again, "only
mind my conditions."

To make a long story short, Billy thramped off and found Jack,
and tould him what the king of the castle was afther saying.

"Well, father," says Jack, says he, "what can't be cured must be
indured, so you'd betther be up betimes in the mornin', an'
come along with me till we meet some daicent thief that's masther of his thrade that you'll 'prentice me to, for between

ourselves I was long *switherin'* to go an' larn the thrade properly anyhow, for though they say that a self-made man is the best,
still in this back'ard place one has to work under a great many
disadvantages in the up-hill part of the business, so that there's
often I would have given my one eye for a couple of good hints
from a purficient in the thrade."

No sooner said than done. Jack and his father took the road
early next mornin', and a weary travel they had of it that day
through a strange country till tor'st night they come to an inn
where there was entertainment for man and baste—and for
boys too—and they put up there that night, and slept sound
I can tell ye, and, moreover, when Billy payed the landlord
the damage next mornin', doesn't my brave Jack stale twicet
as much back again out of the till before he left. Well they
started that morning again and travelled on, and on, of a hot
summer's day, when tor'st evening who did they meet but the
mastherman thief of all that counthry, and there and then
Billy bound over Jack to him for three years; and he gave Jack
his blissin' and told him make the most of his opportunities,
and to always keep before his eyes the fear of what he'd meet
with from the King of Ballyshanny when he'd come back if he
wasn't masther of his trade. Jack promised faithfully that it
wouldn't be his fault or he'd know the ins and the outs of the
business so far as the ould buck that he was 'prenticed to
could put him. Billy then set out for home again, and there
was nothing more heerd of me brave Jack till the three years
was up.

They weren't long in passing, and on the day afther the end of
the three years Jack comes steppin' into his father's house; and
Billy, I can tell you, was delighted to see him. He hardly knew
him, for he had grown to be as fine and able lookin' a man as
you'd meet in the longest day in summer.

"Jack," says his father, says he, throwin' his arms about him,
"have ye larned yer thrade?"

"I hope I have, father," says he.

"Jack, *ahaskey*," says the father, "you know what the king has
promised if ye're not able to do the three things he puts afore
ye?"

"Yes, father," says Jack; "and I'll do my best to do them, and, as yourself says, sure the best can do no more."

Well, that evening the father took Jack up to the castle, and when the king come out he told him that this was Jack come home again afther sarvin' his 'prenticeship, and he had the thrade back with him.

"Why, Jack," says the king, "it's welcome ye are, in troth—*ceud mile failte romhat*—and it's fresh and bloomin' ye're lookin'—what speed did ye come at yer thrade?"

"Why, thank ye kindly, yer highness," says Jack, "I can't complain at all; I think I done very fairly for my time—at laist, that was my masther's opinion, and he's not the worst judge"; for, ye see, Jack was modest and didn't care for puffin' and blowin' about himself.

"Well, it's well for ye, Jack," says the king back to him, "for the three thrials I'll put afore ye will be *no miss,* I assure ye."

"Well, yer kingship," says Jack, "I'll feel honoured to do what I can for ye. Would yer highness be plaised to let me know the first, for it's as well to get the unpleasant business over at wanst?"

"The first thing, Jack, you'll have to do," says the king, "is this: To-morrow morning I'll send out a plough and two horses to plough the tattie field at the back of the hill, and I'll send two men with them, armed to the teeth; and you'll have to stale the two horses out of the plough unknownst to the men, and if ye let to-morrow night fall on ye without having the horses stolen you'll undhergo the punishment for high thrayson—you'll be burned, beheaded, and hung; and this time to-morrow I hope to be feasting my eyes on your head stuck on the porch of that gate there. Do you think will ye be able to succeed, Jack?" says he, laughing hearty.

"Why, yer highness," says Jack, "sure I'll do my best, and the best can do no more."

Jack and his father went home; the father very downhearted entirely, seein' that there didn't seem to be any chance for poor Jack at all; and he thought he'd see him burned, beheaded, and hung before his eyes the next night.

Jack didn't say much, but went to bed and slept sound. He was

up with the lark next mornin', and away out through the fields.
He searched the meadows till he come on a hare asleep, and
catching it he broke one of its legs, and fetched it home with him.
The king sent out the two horses according to his promise to
plough the tattie field, and he sent with them two men armed to
the teeth, and had sthrict ordhers that Jack Brogan would
attempt to stale the horses out of the plough that day, but they
weren't to allow him on the paril of their lives, but were to shoot
him if he thried; and if they allowed him to stale the horses, they
would be hung to the first bush themselves. Well, of course, they
had their eyes about them, and ploughed, and ploughed away till
evening, and no sign of Jack; so they agreed that Jack had too
much wit to run the risk of gettin' shot, that he had given up the
thing in despair, and had gone and dhrownded himself. With that
they sees a hare with a broken leg coming over the ditch, and
away limpin' across the field before them. Whirroo! both of them
throws down their guns and swords and afther that hare for bare
life. They didn't go far till they caught it, but when they come
back the horses was gone, as clane as if they had nivir been there,
and Jack was half roads to the castle with them. He met the king
at the gate and handed him over his horses.

"Well, Jack," said the king—and I can tell you he opened
his eyes wide when he sees Jack marchin' up to him with the
horses—"well, Jack," says he, "ye done that cliverly, but them
rascals have been too slack with ye, and I'll take ye in hands
myself now. The second thing ye'll have to do—and it's no
miss—is to steal the sheet that will be undher myself and the
queen when we are sleeping to-morrow night. I'll keep my hand
on a loaded gun all night, and the first man enthers my room I'll
shoot him dead, and if ye don't succeed in stalin' it, ye know
what'll happen ye. What do you think of that, Jack?"

"Well," says Jack, "I'll do my best, and sure ye know the best
can do no more."

Then the king was off to ordher out his sojers to hang the two
men, and away went Jack home, and you may be sure his father
was proud to see him back safe, but when Jack tould him the
second thrial, he got down-hearted again, and said he'd surely
lose his boy this time.

Jack said nothin', but went to his bed and slept sound that night again; and the next night he went to the graveyard and dug up a fresh corp about the same age as himself, and taking it home he dhressed it in a shoot of his own clothes, and started for the castle in the middle of the night, and gettin' undher the king's bedroom window, he hoisted up the corp, and at the same time threw gravel again the panes.

"What's that?" says the king, jumping up in his bed; and seeing the head at the window he fired, and Jack, with that, let the corp fall.

"Ha, ha," says the king, "I was too able for ye, Jack, my boy; ye're done for at length, and it's yer desarvin'. Now, queen," says he to her ladyship, "I'll have to run out and bury this corp."

Jack waited till he saw the king safe away with the corp, and then he climbed in of the window.

"You weren't long away, king," says her ladyship from the bed.

"Oh," says Jack, purtendin' the king's voice, "I kem back for the sheet to wrap up the corp in an' carry him to the graveyard."

And sure enough, she hands it to him to wrap round the corp, and me brave Jack steps out of the window and away with him.

It wasn't long afther till the king come in with his teeth chattherin', and steps into bed.

"Where's the sheet?" he cried, jumpin' up as soon as he missed it.

"Why, ye *amadan*," says the queen, "didn't ye come back and say you wanted it to wrap up the corp and carry it to the graveyard."

"Oh, Jack—Jack," says the king, lying back in his bed again, "you have thricked me wanst more! But, plaise Providence, that will be the last time."

Next day Jack come to the castle with the sheet rowled up an' ondher his arm, and presented it to the king.

"Well, Jack," says the king, smilin', "ye done me again, but the third time, ye mind, is the charm. To-morrow night I'll sleep with all my clothes, as well as my shoot of mail, on me, and you're to steal this inside shirt (showing it to him) that has my name written on the inside of the breast of it, ye persave, off my back, and leave another shirt on me in its place, and I'll have a loaded gun in every hand all night, and there'll be a senthry at every window in my house, and two at every door, and my bedroom will be filled with sodgers; and if ye don't succeed, ye know what'll happen ye. Eh, what do you think of that, Jack?"

"Why," says Jack, says he, "sure I'll do my best, and the best, ye know, can do no more."

Now Jack's father was jumpin' out of his skin with delight when he found that Jack stole the sheet, but when Jack come home this night, an' tould his father that he had to steal the inside shirt, with the king's name on the inside of the breast, off the king's back, and leave another in its place unknownst to him, while he slept with all his clothes as well as a shoot of mail on him, and a loaded gun in every hand, and with a senthry at every window, and two at every door, and the room full of sodgers, faix Jack's father's heart gave way again entirely, and he said that Jack was as good as lost to him now, anyhow.

Jack said nothing but went to bed and slept sounder now than ever he did, and getting up betimes in the mornin' he went to a tailyer and got him to make a shirt of the same description, and of the very same cloth as the king's inside shirt; and he got the tailyer to prent something in the inside of the breast of it—but what it was we'll not say now. In the middle of the night he rowled up the shirt, and buttoning it up inside his coat, he stharted for the castle. When the senthries seen him comin', they ups with their guns to shoot him, when he shouted out not to mind, for that he was comin' to give himself up, seein' that it was no use in him endayvourin' to do what was onpossible to be done. So, they got round him, and takin' him into the castle, they fetched him to the king's bedroom, where they wakened the king, and told him that Jack had give in at last and couldn't do it.

"Why, Jack," said the king, laughin' hearty, "I knew I would be one too many for ye. Ordher up the hangman at once till we get through with this business."

"Oh, aisy, aisy, if ye plase," said Jack, "sure this was nothin' but a joke of me. I have the shirt already stolen off yer back, and another in its place."

The king swore this was onpossible, and the sojers till a man swore the same, but the king, knowin' Jack was so able, thought it betther not to shout till he was out of the wood; so he pulled off him till he reached the shirt.

"There it is yet, Jack, ye see," says he.

"Is that it?" says Jack. "Is yer name in it?"

"To be sure it is," says the king, readin' it.

"Show me," says Jack; and turnin' round to the light to read the name, purtindin', he slips it undher his coat in the winkin' of a midge's eye, and whips out the other shirt. "Ay, sure enough," says Jack, handin' back *his own,* "that's it all right. So I suppose ye may as well get up the hangman and let us finish off the business at wanst."

"Sartinly, Jack," says the king, gettin' himself into the shirt and clothes again, "sartinly; delays is dangerous."

But, lo and behould you! when the hangman was got and everything was prepared, the king asked Jack if he had anything to say before he'd die.

"Why, yes, yer highness," says Jack, "I have a thriflin' wee word to say."

"An' what is it?" says the king. "Out with it, man, and don't be backward about it."

"Why," says Jack, pullin' out the king's shirt from undher his coat, "it's only this—there's yer shirt stolen off yer back, although ye slept in yer clothes and a shoot of mail, and with a senthry at ivery window, and two at ivery door, and yer bedroom filled with sojers, and I have left another shirt on yer back."

The king looked at the shirt and read his name on it, and, turnin' nine colours at wanst, he peeled off him again, and takin' off his inside shirt he read on the inside of the breast of it:—

> "Sould again, ould brick!
> This is my third thrick—
> The shirt taken off yer back
> By
> MASTHER-THIEF JACK."

The king was thundher-struck, and no wondher! He ups and he says at wanst, just as soon as he got his senses gathered:—

"Jack," says he, "you must lave my dominions, for I'm not sure but ye might stale the very teeth out of my head, if ye only took the notion. I'm sorry, indeed, Jack, but go ye must. At the same time I'll threat ye daicent—ye'll have as much gold with ye as yer pockets can hould."

"Thank ye for nothin'," says Jack back to him, "for I could have that if yer highness was to put it undher all the locks in the kingdom. But I have one requist to ask ye afore I go."

"Name it, Jack," says the king.

"Will ye see that me ould father nivir wants for anything while he lives?"

"Troth, I will that, Jack, for I'll take him up to the castle to live along with myself; he'll get aitin' and dhrinkin' of the best; he'll not be asked to do a hand's turn of work, and he'll be as happy as the day is long."

Jack thanked the king hearty, and set out on his thravels. He went back to the country he was 'prenticed in, and as his ould masther had just died, Jack was appointed Masther-man-thief of that whole counthry, and lived happy and well ivir afther.

# Manis the Besom Man

ONCE ON A TIME when pigs was swine, long, long ago, there was a man named Manis who supported himself and his ould disabled mother by making besoms out of the long heather on the lonely moor where they lived. One day, when Manis was driving a very sorry old institution of a horse—that you could count every bone in his body through his skin—to the town, with a load of besoms for sale, he begun to ruminate to himself on the bad trade this same besom-making was becoming, entirely, that he could hardly keep body and sowl sticking together himself, let alone support his mother and an old horse, that would soon die on his hands anyway; and then he'd be in a fix, for he couldn't scrape as much money together as would buy a new straddle, let alone a new horse. And, as for selling this one, it's what he'd have to pay a man to take him off his hands, let alone get money for him. But it's a bad disaise that can't be cured somehow, Manis said to himself—so he began to consider how he could sell his rickle of a pony to advantage. Manis had about as clever a head as ever was set on ignorant shoulders— and right well he knew this—and he was not long finding a way out of the pickle. When he went to the town and disposed of his besoms, and got the money for them, he put the money into shilling pieces, half-crown pieces, and one half-sovereign, and inquiring for the grandest hotel, he put his horse into the stable, and stuck the gold half-sovereign and all the other pieces into the holes in its hide—for the poor baste's skin had holes enough to hide away a fortune in, goodness knows!—slipping them just what you'd know in under the skin, and then he went into the hotel, and ordered the best of everything, eating and drinking for himself, and as for the horse, he told them not to spare the corn and bran mashes on him, for he was going to put him into training for a great race. Manis got all he called for, and the horse, too, got everything of the best, and that all fared well till it came to the paying of the bill, which reached a big figure entirely. When the bill was put before him, Manis said he would call again and pay it; that he had no ready cash about him now, and all that; but the waiters raised the divil of a ruction, and sent for the owner of the hotel himself, who happened to be Mayor over the town; and they pointed out Manis to him, and told him the whole story, and the Mayor said that if Manis didn't take and pay the money on that instant moment, he would send for the soldiers and have him hung by coort-martial at once.

"Well, well," sez Manis, sez he, "but this is a nice how-do-ye-do, that a gintleman can't be trusted for a few shillings, only this way. Sweet good luck to you and your house," sez he to the Mayor. "I never yet in all my travels met with such ondaicent people. Though I have a shabby coat on me atself," sez Manis, "don't judge me by that, for that's my notion, and it's the way I choose to go. And look ye here now, Misther Mayor," sez he, "I could not only pay for my own dinner, but I could invite every mother's sowl in this town—good, bad, and ondifferent, big, wee, and middling—here, and give them their dinners and pay for them, and buy you out of house and home then, and make a present of the whole consarn to your waiter there the next minute, and live as ondependent as a prence still after," sez Manis. "But if you must be paid for your hungry bit of a dinner that wouldn't break a man's fast on a Good Friday, ye must. I left my purse behind me at home, and I didn't just want to abuse my poor baste now, seeing he's afther a long journey; but to stop your throat I'll do anything, so here goes." And with that Manis plants his hat on his head and away out to the stables, with the Mayor and all the waiters after him to see what he was up to at all, at all.

Manis led out the pony to the yard, and telling the crowd to stand off him, he got the pony by the head with one hand, and with a stick in the other he struck the horse's ribs just beside the place he hid the half-sovereign, and the horse flung up as well as he was able—bekase for six years afore he never had the spirit to fling till he got the feed of corn and bran—and out jumps the goold half-sovereign, and rolls just right to the Mayor's feet. The Mayor looked down at it bewildered.

"Will ye kindly," sez Manis, sez he, in an offhand sort of way to the Mayor, "will yer Mayorship kindly pick up that coin and tell me how much it is?"

The Mayor picked it up, and he looked at it, and he turned it over and looked at the other side, and then jingled it on the ground, and next bit it with his teeth.

"Well, by all that's infarnal," sez he, "but it's a good shining goold half-sovereign," sez he, "with the King's head on it."

"Humph!" sez Manis, sez he, "is that all? That's not enough then, we must try again."

So Manis whacked the horse again, and again, and again; and the horse flung up again, and again, and again; and the coins come jumping out, rolling among the waiters, and them picking them up and shouting out every time how much they were. When Manis got enough to pay the bill——

"Now," sez he, "when I have my hand on him, I may as well take the price of a box of matches and a bit of tobacco out of him," and he flogged out another couple of half-crowns, the Mayor and the waiters looking on with their mouths open and rubbing their eyes every now and then to see whether it was asleep or awake they were. When Manis had finished, and had all the pieces flogged out of him except a couple, he yoked him into the cart as if he was going to start.

"I say, my good man," sez the Mayor, when he got his breath with him—"I say, my good man," sez he, "would you sell that horse?"

"Is it sell him?" sez Manis, sez he. "Not by no means."

"I would be content to give you a good penny for him," sez the Mayor; "just as a cur'osity to show my friends, you know."

"You'll have to get some other cur'osity for your friends this time, then," sez Manis. "This would be a rare cur'osity, entirely."

"I wouldn't refuse you fifty pounds down in cold cash for him," sez the Mayor.

"Faix, I suppose you would not," sez Manis, tartly.

"I wouldn't refuse you a hundred pounds down for him, now that I think of it," sez the Mayor.

"Think again," sez Manis.

"Oh, but I considher that a big penny," sez the Mayor.

"And wouldn't you considher five hundred, bigger?" sez Manis.

"Oh, I couldn't think of that, my good man," sez the Mayor.

"Very well and good, then," replied Manis. "When every one sticks to his own, no man's wronged. Good morning and good luck" sez he, pretending to go and to drive off.

"Hold on ye," sez the Mayor, running forward and catching the reins. "Is it very expensive, his keep? Have you to feed him on anything special to get them coins out of him?"

"Yes, sartintly," sez Manis, "his keep is a very expensive item entirely, and if you're not purpared to give him his fill of good oat, corn, and bran, there's no use in you throwing away your hard-earned money purchasing him from me. I like to be honest with you, so good morning again."

"Hold on you! Hold on, you!" sez the Mayor, pulling the reins with all his might, for Manis was making wonderful big quivers with the reins and the whip as if he wanted to get away whither or no, and that he was no way consarned to make sale.

"Hold on, you!" sez the Mayor. "One of you run in there," sez he to the waiters, "and fetch me out five-hundred pounds you'll get rolled up in the foot of an old stocking in the bottom corner of my trunk, and the others of you take this horse out of the cart and put him into the stable," sez he.

So the waiter soon come running back with the foot of an old stocking, and the Lord Mayor counted five hundred goold sovereigns out of it down into Manis's hand, and Manis and him parted, Manis going whistling home with a light heart.

The Mayor had the pony locked up in a stable by itself, up to the eyes in corn and bran, and he double-locked it, putting the key into his own pocket, and then went round the town telling all his gentlemen friends of his good fortune, and inviting them all to come at twelve o'clock the next day till they would have the pleasure of seeing him flogging a hundhred pound or so out of

the horse. Sure enough, at twelve o'clock the next day, all his
gentlemen friends were gathered in the hotel yard, and the
Lord Mayor come out and opened the stable door, and ordered
one of his men in to lead out the horse. He was provided with a
nice little tough cane himself, that he had bought at eighteen-
pence in a little shop next doore, specially for the occasion, and
he ordered his man to lead the horse into the middle of the yard,
and then he went round clearing a circle about the horse,
putting his gentlemen friends back with the cane, as he said the
little coins would likely be rolling among them, and would
maybe get lost.

"Now, John," says he to the man who was holding the horse,
"keep a good tight grip on the reins, and don't let him burst
away. I'll not keep you long, for I'll only take a few hundhred
pounds or so out of him the day, just to let these gentlemen
friends of mine see the thing. Hold hard, now," sez he, and he
drew the cane a sharp slap on the poor baste's ribs.

Up flung the horse, and out jumped a coin, and rolled into the
crowd.

The Lord Mayor crossed his arms, and axed some of the
crowd to lift it and tell him what was it.

They lifted and examined it, as if it was one of the seven wonders of the world, and they bit it, and scratched it, and jingled it,
an sez they——

"It's a good, bright shilling, with the king's head on it."

"Humph!" sez the Lord Mayor, a wee bit taken back, "Is that
all? I expected a bit of goold, but the goold's to come yet. Hold
hard again, John!" sez he, and he come down another sharp rap
on the horse's ribs. Up flung the horse, and out jumps another
coin. "Kindly tell me," sez he, crossing his arms, and looking on
indifferently—"kindly tell me," sez he, "how much is that?"

The crowd took it up again, and scratched it, and rubbed it,
and jingled it, and bit it, and sez they——

"It's a half-crown, by the toss o' war!"

"Well, middling, middling," says he, "we're getting towards
the goold now. Hold hard again, John! Look out, gentlemen, for
I'm guessing this will be a half-sovereign, or a sovereign, and it
might get lost." And with that he comes down another rap on

the baste's ribs, but lo and behold you, though the horse flung ever so high, the sorra take the coin or coin come out.

The Lord Mayor looked round him, and then looked up in the air to see if the coin went up that way, and forgot to come down; but seeing no sign of it there, he turned to John, and sez he——

"What way did that coin go, John?"

"Faith," sez John, sez he, "you put me a puzzle. Ax me another."

"There's some mistake," says the Lord Mayor, squaring himself out, and folding up his sleeves. "I'm afeard I didn't strike hard enough that time; but it will not be my fault this time or I will." So down he comes such a polthogue on the poor brute's bones as made its inside sound like a drum, and up higher than ever the baste flung its heels, and the Lord Mayor and John, and all the crowd stood back to watch for the coin, but good luck to their wit! if they were watching from that time till this the dickens receive the coin or coin would they see.

"Right enough," sez the Lord Mayor, sez he, "it's as plain as a pike staff that there must be some mistake here. Don't you think isn't there some mistake, John?"

"Faix," sez John, "I would be very strongly of the opinion that there is."

"John," sez the Lord Mayor, sez he, "I think we're not holding his head the right way. It strikes me that the owner of him held his head north when he was flogging the money out of him. What do you think if we hold his head north?"

"Anything at all you plaise," sez John, "I'm paid to obey orders."

"All right then, John, just move his head round that way a little. That's it. That will do," sez the Lord Mayor. "Now hold hard, John, and keep a sharp eye out for the coin," sez he, spitting on the stick and winding it round his head, and fetching it down, oh, melia murdher! that you'd think it wouldn't leave a bone in the poor baste's body it wouldn't knock into stirabout. And then up flung the horse, and the Mayor jumped back, and they all jumped back, and then the Mayor held out his hand and said, "Whisht! Whisht!" an set up his ears to hear where the coin would fall; but, movrone, ne'er a coin or coin was to be heard.

The first thing the Mayor heard was a bit of a titter of a laugh, and then another and another, till the titter went round all his gintlemen friends. With that he got black in the face, to find he had made such a fool of himself, and to the flogging of the horse he falls again, determined to have it out of him if there was a coin at all in him. And he flogged him high up and low down, and all around, whacking and striking, and puffing, and cursing, and the baste flinging and leaping, and neighing, and whinnying, till at length ye a'most wouldn't see the poor animal for blood and foam. And his gintlemen friends round about had to interfare at last, and drag him away from the horse by brute force, and threaten to give him in charge to the soldiers if he didn't stop murdering the creature, and the horse was dragged off and the Lord Mayor was dragged in, and the whole town laughed for nine days after till they laughed the Lord Mayor clean out of his office. And as for Manis, the rascal, he give up the besom-making trade, as well he might, and he lived an ondependent private jintleman, himself and his mother, for the rest of their days, on the intherest of his money.

# Jack and the King
# Who Was a Gentleman

IT IS MUCH to be regretted that the Bummadier was not a millionaire; for in that case, at the Bocht money would run like the rain at Lammas. Of course, with a steady and assured income of two pounds five shillings and sixpence per quarter, he was rich enough to be generous—but, alas, not rich enough to be lavish.

There was no other employer of labour at the Bocht to whom the youngsters would give their services with the alacrity they ever showed when the Bummadier had a cart of fir to take in, or rushes to bear home from the Bottoms, to thatch his cabin. And, awaiting their promised pennies, they, in course of time, got to know Pay-day, and to long for it with all the greedy eagerness of the thirstiest old pensioner in the land.

But, in consideration of Pay-day being still far in the future, Corney was frequently importuned by his mercenaries to acknowledge their drafts, and pay interest thereon, in the shape of a good exciting story of the King's-and-Queen's age. Which demands, that he might stave off a run on the bank, the Bummadier was fain to concede. For the Widow's Pat, these tales had a thrilling interest, and on the occasion of one, seated in his usual *siostog* in the corner, he followed it with such breathless excitement as held not even the youngsters themselves.

Well, children: wanst upon a time, when pigs was swine, there was a poor widdy woman lived all alone with her wan son Jack in a wee hut of a house, that on a dark night ye might aisily walk over it by mistake, not knowin' at all, at all, it was there, barrin' ye'd happen to strike yer toe again' it. An' Jack an' his mother lived for lee an' long, as happy as hard times would allow them, in this wee hut of a house, Jack sthrivin' to 'arn a little support for them both by workin' out, an' doin' wee turns back an' forrid to the neighbours. But there was one winter, an' times come to look black enough for them—nothin' to do, an' less to ate, an' clothe themselves as best they might; an' the winther wore on, getting' harder an' harder, till at length when Jack got up out of his bed on a mornin', an' axed his mother to make ready the drop of stirabout for their little brakwus as usual, "Musha, Jack, *a mhic*," says his mother, says she, "the male-chist—thanks be to the Lord!—is as empty as Paddy Ruadh's donkey that used to ate his brakwus at supper-time. It stood out long an' well, but it's empty at last, Jack, an' no sign of how we're goin' to get it filled again—only we trust in the good Lord that niver yet disarted the widow and the orphan—He'll not see us wantin', Jack."

"The Lord helps them that help themselves, mother," says Jack back again to her.

"Thrue for ye, Jack," says she, "but I don't see how we're goin' to help ourselves."

"He's a mortial dead mule out an' out that hasn't a kick in him," says Jack. "An', mother, with the help of Providence—not comparin' the Christian to the brute baste—I have a kick in me yet; if you thought ye could only manage to sthrive along the best way you could for a week, or maybe two weeks, till I get back again off a little journey I'd like to undhertake."

"An' may I make bould to ax, Jack," says his mother to him, "where would ye be afther makin' the little journey to?"

"You may that, then, Mother," says Jack. "It's this: You know the King of Munsther is a great jintleman entirely. It's put on him, he's so jintlemanly, that he was niver yet known to make use of a wrong or disrespectable word. An' he prides himself on it so much that he has sent word over all the known airth that he'll give his beautiful daughter—the loveliest picthur in all Munsther, an' maybe in all Irelan', if we'd say it—an' her weight in goold, to any man that in three trials will make him use the unrespectful word, an' say, 'Ye're a liar!' But every man that tries

him, an' fails, loses his head. All sorts and descriptions of people, from prences an' peers down to bagmen an' beggars, have
come from all parts of the known world to thry for the great
prize, an' all of them up to this has failed, an' by consequence
lost their heads. But, mother dear," says Jack, "where's the use
in a head to a man if he can't get mail for it to ate? So I'm goin'
to thry me fortune, only axin' your blissin' an' God's blissin' to
help me on the way."

"Why, Jack, a *thaisge*," says his mother, "it's a dangersome
task; but as you remark, where's the good of the head to ye when
ye can't get mail to put in it? So, I give ye my blissin', an' night,
noon, an' mornin' I'll be prayin' for ye to prosper."

An' Jack set out, with his heart as light as his stomach, an' his
pocket as light as them both together; but a man 'ill not travel
far in ould Irelan' (thanks be to God!) on the bare-footed stomach—as we'll call it—or it'll be his own fault if he does; an' Jack
didn't want for plenty of first-class aitin' an' dhrinkin' lashin's an'
laivin's, and pressin' him to more. An' in this way he thravelled
away afore him for five long days till he come to the King of
Munsther's castle. And when he was comed there he rattled on
the gate, an' out come the King.

"Well, me man," says the King, "what might be your business
here?"

"I'm come here, your Kingship," says Jack, mighty polite, an'
pullin' his forelock, be raison his poor ould mother had always
insthructed him in the heighth of good breedin'—"I'm come
here, your R'yal Highness," says Jack, "to thry for yer daughter."

"Hum!" says the King. "Me good young man," says he, "don't
ye think it a poor thing to lose yer head?"

"If I lose it," says Jack, "sure one consolation 'ill be that I'll
lose it in a glorious cause."

An' who do ye think would be listenin' to this same deludherin'
speech of Jack's, from over the wall, but the King's beautiful
daughter herself. She took an eyeful out of Jack, an' right well
plaised she was with his appearance, for——

"Father," says she at once, "hasn't the boy as good a right to
get a chance as another? What's his head to you? Let the boy in,"
says she.

An' sure enough, without another word, the King took Jack within the gates, an' handin' him over to the sarvints, tould him to be well looked afther an' cared for till mornin'.

Next mornin' the King took Jack with him an' fetched him out into the yard. "Now then, Jack," says he, "we're goin' to begin. We'll drop into the stables here, an' I'll give you your first chance."

So he took Jack into the stables an' showed him some wondherful big horses, the likes of which poor Jack never saw afore, an' everyone of which was the heighth of the side wall of the castle an' could step over the castle walls, which were twenty-five feet high, without strainin' themselves.

"Them's purty big horses, Jack," says the King. "I don't suppose ever ye saw as big or as wondherful as them in yer life."

"Oh, they're purty big indeed," says Jack, takin' it as cool as if there was nothin' whatsomever astonishin' to him about them. "They're purty big indeed," says Jack, *for this counthry*. But at home with us in Donegal we'd only count them little nags, shootable for the young ladies to dhrive in ponycarriages."

"What!" says the King, "do ye mane to tell me ye have seen bigger in Donegal?"

"Bigger!" says Jack. "Phew! Blood alive, yer Kingship, I seen horses in my father's stable that could step over your horses without thrippin'. My father owned one big horse—the greatest, I believe, in the world again."

"What was he like?" says the King.

"Well, yer Highness," says Jack, "it's quite beyond me to tell ye what he was like. But I know when we wanted to mount it could only be done by means of a step-laddher, with nine hundred and ninety steps to it, every step a mile high, an' you had to jump seven mile off the topmost step to get on his back. He ate nine ton of turnips, nine ton of oats, an' nine ton of hay, in the day an' it took ninety-nine men in the day-time, an' ninety-nine more in the night-time, carrying his feeds to him; an' when he wanted a drink, the ninety-nine men had to lead him to a lough that was nine mile long, nine mile broad, an' nine mile deep, an' he used to drink it dry every time," says Jack, an' then he looked at the King, expectin' he'd surely have to make a liar of him for that.

But the King only smiled at Jack, an' says he, "Jack, that was a wonderful horse entirely, an' no mistake."

Then he took Jack with him out into the garden for his second trial, an' showed him a bee-skep, the size of the biggest rick of hay ever Jack had seen; an' every bee in the skep was the size of a thrush, an' the queeny bee as big as a jackdaw.

"Jack," says the King, says he, "isn't them wondherful bees? I'll warrant ye, ye never saw anything like them?"

"Oh, they're middlin'—middlin' fairish," says Jack—*"for this counthry.* But they're nothin' at all to the bees we have in Donegal. If one of our bees was flying across the fields," says Jack, "and one of your bees happened to come in its way, an' fall into our bee's eye, our bee would fly to the skep, an' ax another bee to take the mote out of his eye."

"Do you tell me so, Jack?" says the King. "You must have great monsthers of bees."

"Monsthers," says Jack. "Ah, yer Highness, monsthers is no name for some of them. I remimber," says Jack, says he, "a mighty great breed of bees me father owned. They were that big that when my father's new castle was a-buildin' (in the steddin' of the old one which he consaived to be too small for a man of his mains), and when the workmen closed in the roof, it was found there was a bee inside, an' the hall door not bein' wide enough, they had to toss the side wall to let it out. Then the queeny bee—ah! she was a wondherful baste entirely!" says Jack. "Whenever she went out to take the air she used to overturn all the ditches and hedges in the country; the wind of her wings tossed houses and castles; she used to swallow whole flower gardens; an' one day she flew against a ridge of mountains nineteen thousand feet high and knocked a piece out from top to bottom, an' it's called Barnesmore Gap to this day. This queeny bee was a great trouble an' annoyance to my father, seein' all the harm she done the naybours round about; and once she took it in her head to fly over to England, an' she created such mischief an' disolation there that the King of Englan' wrote over to my father if he didn't come immaidiately an' take

home his queeny bee that was wrackin' an' ruinin' all afore her
he'd come over himself at the head of all his army and wipe my
father off the face of the airth. So my father ordhered me to
mount our wondherful big horse that I tould ye about, an' that
could go nineteen mile at every step, an' go over to Englan' an'
bring home our queeny bee. An' I mounted the horse an' started,
an' when I come as far as the sea I had to cross to get over to
Englan', I put the horse's two fore feet into my hat, an' in that
way he thrashed the sea dry all the way across an' landed me
safely. When I come to the King of Englan' he had to supply me
with nine hundred and ninety-nine thousand men an' ninety-
nine thousand mile of chains an' ropes to catch the queeny bee
an' bind her. It took us nine years to catch her, nine more to tie
her, an' nine years and nine millions of men to drag her home,
an' the King of Englan' was a beggar afther from that day till the
day of his death. Now what do ye think of that bee?" says Jack,
thinkin' he had the King this time sure enough.

But the King was a cuter one than Jack took him for, an' he
only smiled again, an' says he——

"Well, Jack, that was a wondherful great queeny bee entirely."

Next, for poor Jack's third an' last chance, the King took him
to show him a wondherful field of beans he had, with every
bean-stalk fifteen feet high an' every bean the size of a goose's
egg.

"Well, Jack," says the King says he, "I'll engage ye never saw
more wondherful bean-stalks than them?"

"Is it them?" says Jack. "Arrah, man, yer Kingship," says he,
"they may be very good—*for this counthry;* but sure we'd throw
them out of the ground for useless afther-shoots in Donegal. I
mind one bean-stalk in partickler, that my father had for a show
an' a cur'osity, that he used to show as a great wondher entirely
to sthrangers. It stood on ninety-nine acres of ground, it was
nine hundred mile high, an' every leaf covered nine acres. It fed
nine thousand horses, nine thousand mules, an' nine thousand
jackasses for nineteen years. He used to send nine thousand
harvestmen up the stalk in spring to cut and gather off the soft
branches at the top. They used to cut these off when they'd
reach up as far as them (which was always in the harvest time),

an' throw them down, an' nine hundred and ninety-nine horses an' carts were kept busy for nine months carting the stuff away. Then the harvestmen always reached down to the foot of the stalk at Christmas again."

"Faix, Jack," says the King, "it was a wondherful bean-stalk, that, entirely."

"You might say that," says Jack, trying to make the most of it, for he was now on his last leg. "You might say that," says he. "Why, I mind one year I went up the stalk with the harvestmen, an' when I was nine thousand mile up, doesn't I miss my foot, and down I come. I fell feet foremost, and sunk up to my chin in a whinstone rock that was at the foot. There I was in a quand-hary—but I was not long ruminatin' till I hauled out my knife, an' cut off my head, an' sent it home to look for help. I watched after it, as it went away, an' lo an' behould ye, afore it had gone half a mile I saw a fox set on it, and begin to worry it. 'By this an' by that,' says I to meself, 'but this is too bad!'—an' I jumped out an' away as hard as I could run, to the assistance of my head. An' when I come up, I lifted my foot, an' give the fox three kicks, an' knocked three kings out of him—every one of them a nicer an' a better jintleman than you."

"Ye're a liar, an' a rascally liar," says the King.

"More power to ye!" says Jack, givin' three buck leaps clean into the air, "an' it's proud I am to get you to confess it; for I have won yer daughter."

Right enough the King had to give up to Jack the daughter—an' be the same token, from the first time she clapped her two eyes on Jack she wasn't the girl to gainsay him—an' her weight in goold. An' they were both of them marrid, an' had such a weddin' as surpassed all the weddin's ever was heerd tell of afore or since in that country or in this. An' Jack lost no time in sendin' for his poor ould mother, an' neither herself nor Jack ever after knew what it was to be in want. An' may you an' I never know that same naither.

# The Giant of the Band-beggars' Hall

ONCE UPON A TIME when there were plenty of Kings and Queens in Ireland—it's many of them often we heard of, but few of them ever we seen, except in dhrawin's and picthurs—there was a King and a Queen, and they had one son called Jack. Now, this Jack, when he grew up, was a fine, strong, strapping, able fellow, and he was very fond of fishing. There was one river in particular, alive with trout and fishes of all descriptions, that Jack would never be tired fishing in, but at length the trouts and other fishes in this river begun to get so old-fashioned for him that when they'd find him fishing on one side of the river they would all swim to the other side; and then when my poor Jack would take a boat and cross over to the other side after them, back they'd all swim, and be at the opposite side again by the time he'd have got to the far bank, and they'd then commence wagging their tails, the creatures, out of the water at him tauntingly. Well, it wasn't in human nature to stand that sort of thing; no more was it in Jack, for Jack, of course, was only human; and then Jack would come home in the evening in the very devil of a temper, and maybe commence kicking the cat out of spite, bekase the trouts wagged their tails at him. So this, of course, more or less vexed the King and the Queen, and they put their heads together and had long confabs, consulting what they could do to mollify poor Jack; but the short and the long of it was, they agreed, let it cost what it might, that a bridge must be built over the river for Jack, so that he would be across the river and back before the trouts could have time to get up their tails and wag them. Well, the very next day after this conclusion was come to, all the masons in the country were got together and the bridge built. Early the next morning Jack was up and out, and swearing that there would be no more tails wagged at him or he'd know the reason why. But lo and behold you! when he come to the place where the bridge was put up the day afore, there wasn't two stones of it a-top of other; it was tumbled to the ground and scattered aist and waist, and there didn't seem to be a trout in the river but was gathered to the place, and as soon as Jack put in an appearance ye would think they were wagging their tails for a wager. Jack turned and went home, and he met the cat on the hall-door steps, and he hit her a kick that knocked her clean through the bottom of a new oaken milk-tub his mother had out on the steps airing.

"Well, Jack," sez the King, "surely the trouts aren't wagging their tails at you this morning, now that we have built ye that beautiful new bridge, that there isn't the like of it in the country again?"

"Aren't they though?" sez Jack, sez he. "It's a nice show, your bridge is, this morning, if ye'd be so kind as to go out and look at it, and see how there isn't the second stone of it together, and it's the trouts that know it—the sweet sorra," sez he, "seize the little sowls of the rascals; I never saw them going through such tantrums; it's what one old boyo of a trout that I have had my eye on for the last month curled his tail actually round to his nose," sez he, "and winked his eye out at me," sez he.

"Ye don't tell me so, Jack?" sez the King. "Well, well, this is a purty how d'ye do. Well, Jack," sez he, "I suppose there's no use crying over spilt masonry, no more nor spilt milk, and all we can do is call the masons together again, and build it up."

So, called together they were, and the bridge was up again afore night. And my brave Jack was up with the lark in the morning, and down to the river with his rod, but oh, sorra seize the bridge or bridge was there! It was scattered to the four winds; and the trouts, the scoundhrils, they were ten times more provoking then ever, actually standing on their heads with delight. There was no holding of Jack this morning. He came back from the river in the very mischief of a temper, and not meeting with the cat this time—for she found him coming back—he lifted the milk-tub that his mother had got a new bottom in since, and knocked it clean through the hall-door and the partition beyond, into the parlour where the King and the Queen were sitting at breakfast, scattering the table and the fine spread of pancakes and tea all over the room.

"Oh, Jack, Jack," sez the King, sez he, coming rushing out— "Jack, Jack," sez he; "calm yourself, calm yourself. You have frightened your poor mother out of a year's growth, and spoiled her nice pancakes on her."

"Oh, pancakes be rammed!" sez Jack.

"Jack, Jack," sez the King, sez he; "what——what's the matter this morning? Surely that old trout hasn't been putting his tail to his nose this morning again? If he has," sez he, "trust me but I'll soon have him taught a trick worth two of that. He must be let know who's master and who's man here, and that he can't treat the King's son with disrespect."

"Oh," sez Jack, sez he, "I wish you'd just go down and look at thon bridge of yours this morning again, maybe ye'd find reason to understand then, that not the King's son, but the King himself is treated with disrespect and contempt."

"Jack," sez the King, taken aback, "surely, Jack," sez he, "ye don't mean to insinuate that the bridge is down again?"

"Don't I though?" sez Jack, with a sneer.

"Well," sez the King, shaking his head, and looking at the ground—"well," sez he, "that flogs the divil."

"I'll tell you what it is," sez Jack. "You put up the bridge once more, and leave the rest of it to me; if it comes down again I'll be able to give an account of myself, and I'll make some devil dance to a tune he didn't call for."

"The third time's the charm," sez the King; "and the third time it will go up, Jack. Then I'll leave the rest of it to you."

So, up it went the third time, and that night Jack determined to sit up and watch the bridge. All went well till about close on midnight, when, Jack being nodding asleep on the bridge, he found it shaking. Up he jumps, and down he runs under the bridge to see what was wrong with it, or who was shaking it, and there, och, och! he beheld the greatest Giant he ever saw in his life afore.

"Who are you?" sez the Giant, ready to devore Jack.

"I am the King's son, Jack," sez Jack, sez he.

"Well," sez the Giant, "all rights to this river belong to me, and the King should not have built a bridge over it. By right," sez he, "I should take your life now; but I see," sez he, "you're a smart, clean, active-looking boy, and would be sarviceable to me; and as I never yet took unfair advantage of an enemy, it's not worth my while commencing on you," sez the Giant, sez he, "so I'll give you a chance for your life," sez he. "Here's a pack of cards, now," sez he, producing a pack, "and I'll play you a fair game. If you win, you'll get your life, and I'll let the bridge remain, but if I win I'll either take your life on the spot or put a condition on you. Do you agree to that?"

"Done," sez Jack, for he thought to himself it would be all the one anyhow, whether he agreed to it or not.

"What game will it be?" sez the Giant.

"Short, and be done with it; we'll make it twenty-five," sez Jack.

"All right," sez the Giant, "cut for deal."

Jack cut and won the deal. He shuffled and dealt them, turned a five and won three tricks.

"That's sharp for me, Jack," says the Giant, as he shuffled.

Jack got a slashing hand again. Spades was trumps, and Jack led with the ace, but the big fellow covered with the ace of hearts, raised again with the fingers of trumps, and followed up with the knave, a twinkle in his eye all the time.

Jack threw down his cards.

"Ha, ha! Jack," says the Giant. "too able for ye? Eh? No odds though," sez he; "you're not a bad hand at the flats, and have a deal of spunk in you, so I'll give ye a chance for your life yet."

"What's that?" sez Jack.

"It's this," says the Giant. "Within a year and a day from this you're to find out my castle, where I live when I'm at home: but if you're not able to find it, then I'll have your life, toss this bridge, and leave the highest stone in your father's castle the lowest."

"And who are you?" sez Jack.

Sez the Giant——

"I'm the Giant of the Band-beggars' Hall,
The greatest Giant over them all."

"I have never heard of your castle," sez Jack.

"Nor I hope never will," sez the Giant.

"Well, that's to be seen," says Jack.

So the Giant and he parted, and Jack went home—for it was now morning—and told the King and Queen all that had happened. They were greatly vexed entirely, and cursed it for a misfortunate bridge, and tried to persuade Jack to remain at home and not go away on such a wild-goose chase, to the Lord knows where, looking for

"The Giant of the Band-beggars' Hall,
The greatest Giant over them all."

But Jack wasn't to be persuaded, and whether or why, he would go, and never rest till he would find him out, or else lose his life. So he spit on his stick, and, taking his father's and mother's blessing, started off that very day. And Jack travelled afore him for months, without ever once stopping, or eating a bite, or sleeping a wink; and at nightfall one day, he came to a great castle on a lonely moor in the Eastern World, and he went in and saw a Giant sitting by the fire. When Jack came in, the Giant got up, and sez he——

"You're very welcome, Jack, the King of Ireland's son, for I haven't seen the face of a Christian for the last three hundred years."

Jack wondered how he knew his name, but he didn't say anything. The Giant then put Jack sitting by a roaring fire, and taking a knife he cut down the quarter of a rat that was hung in the smoke of the chimney and roasted it on the coals, and himself and Jack made a hearty supper of it, and then each of them slept on a harrow with a goatskin under them and another over them, and Jack slept hearty and well, for he was very tired entirely. Next morning he rose as fresh as a butterfly, and after breakfasting on another quarter of the rat, sez the Giant, sez he——

"I didn't ask you, Jack—where were you going?"

"No more you might," sez Jack; "I might tell you where I'm coming from, but where I'm going is more than I knows."

So Jack starts and he tells him the whole story about him and the Giant of the Band-beggars' Hall. And then he asked him if he could give him any tidings of where he lived?

"Well, no," sez the Giant, "I heard of him only, and that was all. But I'll tell you what I'll do," sez he. "I have command of a third of the birds of the air, and it's likely some of them may know something about him, and if they do I'll soon find it out for you," sez he.

So with that he blew a whistle, and immediately from all corners of the sky the birds begun for to gather, and very soon they were all round the castle, making the sky dark. Then the Giant put it to them did they know anything of——

"The Giant of the Band-beggars' Hall,
The greatest Giant over them all."

or where he lived.

But no, they said they heard tell of him only, but none of them ever reached where he lived.

"Well," sez the Giant, sez he to Jack, "it's bad enough. But I'll tell you what," sez he. "I'll give you a pair of nine-mile boots, and with them you'll reach an older brother of mine who lives a long ways off entirely, and he has command over half the birds of the air, and maybe he could do something for you."

Jack thanked him, and putting on the boots he started away and travelled on, and on, and on, nine mile at every step, till late at night he reached the Giant's older brother's castle away on a very lonely moor, and going in he saw the Giant sitting by the fire. The Giant got up and he says——

"You're welcome Jack, the King of Ireland's son, for I haven't seen the face of a Christian for six hundred years. You stopped at my brother's house last night," sez he.

"I did," sez Jack, all the time wondering how he knew him, or where he stopped last night, but he said nothing.

Then the Giant put Jack beside the big fire, and cutting down two quarters of a rat that was hung in the smoke of the chimney, he roasted them, and Jack and he ate a quarter a piece, and then they went to bed, everyone of them on a harrow, with a goatskin under them and another over them; and Jack slept well and sound for he was very tired, and got up as fresh as a butterfly in the morning, and when they had eaten a good breakfast of the other half of the rat the Giant asked Jack where was he going.

"Well," sez Jack, sez he, "I might tell you how far I come, but I can't tell you how far I am going," and he ups and he tells this Giant the whole story too.

"Well," sez the Giant, sez he, "it's bad enough, but I'll do all I can to help you. I heard tell of the Giant of the Band-beggars' Hall, and that's all I know about him; but I have command over half the birds of the air, and it's likely some of them may know something about him, and if they do I'll soon find out."

So he took out a little whistle and blew it, and in a minute the sky commenced to darken with great flocks of birds flying from all corners, and they all gathered round the Giant's castle. Then the Giant, he put the question to them, if any of them in their travels had come across the Giant of the Band-beggars' Hall,

"The Giant of the Band-beggars' Hall,
The greatest Giant over them all."

But none of them had ever come across him. They had heard tell of him, they said, but that was all.

"Well, it's bad enough," sez the Giant to Jack, "but there's one other remedy yet. I'll lend you a pair of nine-league boots; and I have a brother lives a day's journey from here, by them, who has command over all the birds of the air, and maybe he'll be able to help you."

So off Jack set in the nine-league boots, and late that night he reached the third Giant's house. When he went in, he saw the Giant sitting by the fire, and he got up and welcomed Jack.

"You're welcome, Jack," sez he, "the King of Ireland's son, for I haven't seen the face of a Christian for the last nine hundred years. You slept at my brother's house last night."

Then he sat Jack down by the fire, and reaching up the chimney he took down a rat that was hanging in the smoke, and roasting it on the fire, himself and Jack made a hearty supper of it. And they went to bed, each of them lying on a harrow, with a goat-skin over them and one under them. And Jack slept well and sound, and got up in the morning as fresh as a butterfly. And after they had made a good breakfast on another rat, sez the Giant, sez he——

"Jack, may I ask you how far you intend going?"

"Well," sez Jack, sez he, "I may tell you how far I come, but as to how far I'm going it's more nor I could tell."

So he starts and he tells the Giant the whole story, and he then asked him if he could give him any information as to where the Giant of the Band-beggars' Hall lived?

"Well, no," sez the Giant, sez he, "I heard tell of the Giant of the Band-beggars' Hall, but that was all. But I'll tell you what I'll do," sez the Giant. "I have command of all the birds of the air, and I'll call them together to see if they would know anything about him."

So the Giant blew a whistle, and in a minute the sky was darkened by all the birds of the air gathering together from all corners. And when they were all gathered over the castle the Giant put it to them—Did any of them know anything of

> "The Giant of the Band-beggars' Hall,
> The greatest Giant over them all."

But, lo and behold ye, not one of them knew a thing about him; they had heard tell of him, they said, but none of them ever reached to where he lived.

Poor Jack got into bad heart at this intelligence.

"What will I do now," sez Jack, sez he, to the Giant, "for I'm done now, out and out?"

"I don't know, Jack," sez the Giant. "But hold," sez he, "on second thoughts there's one eagle that isn't here. He flies everywhere over the whole known world, and only comes here to see me once in seven years, and I'm expecting him to-day, for it's just seven years this day since he was with me before. Wait till we see, when he comes, if he has any tidings of him; and if he hasn't I don't know what you'll do."

And sure enough, that very evening they saw the monstrous big eagle—the like of it, for size, Jack never saw before—coming in a thundercloud, darkening the very sky with its wings; and when the Giant saw this, sez he——

"Now, Jack," sez he, "it will not do to let you be seen by the eagle, for he would eat any human being he would see, especially now, when he is coming home ravenous after his big fly."

So he sewed Jack up in a big leathern bag, and hung him by the side of the chimney. And as soon as the eagle had come, the Giant welcomed him and asked him if there was any news.

"No," sez the eagle very sharp, "where would I get news? I'm dead with hunger," sez he; "and get me something to eat at once. It will be better for me than gossiping news with you."

So the Giant went and fetched in a bullock and twelve lambs; and the eagle fell to at once and ate them, bones and all; and he then put his head into his wings and went asleep at once. And the Giant went to bed, too; and Jack was still in the leathern bag, listening to and watching all that was going on. It was late the next morning when the eagle awoke after his big feed. When he did he called for breakfast, and the Giant fetched him in another bullock and twelve lambs, and he ate these up quickly, bones and all; and when he had finished he stroked down his breast with his beak, and flapped his wings two or three times.

"Now," sez he, "I'm myself again."

"Do ye know," sez the Giant, sez he to him, "do ye know, or have ye met in all your travels, the Giant of the Band-beggars' Hall?"

"What would I know about him?" sez the eagle. Then, sez he, "I was there once, but I'll never go there again, for it's away out of the world entirely."

"Well," sez the Giant, "he was here lately, and he left that bag to be sent to his place, and he is to behead me if I don't get it there."

"Well, I'll not take it," sez the eagle.

"Very well, then," sez the Giant, "I suppose I must wait on my fate."

At last, after some time, the eagle sez, sez he——

"Well, you know, I'm under an obligation to you and your

family, and I couldn't refuse you anything; so, I suppose I must take it."

So the Giant took the bag into a room; to sew a burst that was in it, he told the eagle. Then he put in with Jack as much provisions as would last him for a twelve-month. He bid Jack goodbye and wished him God-speed. And Jack heartily thanked him. He then sewed up the bag again and gave it to the eagle. He took it up and started away on his flight, and he flew on, and on, and on, till the days turned to weeks, and the weeks to months, and poor Jack thought they would never reach their journey's end. But at length, when they were nearly a year out—though it seemed to Jack to be twenty years since they started—Jack found the eagle slackening in his flight, and coming down, and down, and down, lower and lower, till at length they touched ground, and Jack cut a little hole in the bag to look out of, and there he saw a castle far greater than all the castles put together that ever he had seen before, and out of it there comes a great Giant, and when Jack saw him he didn't know whether to be glad or sorry, for it was no other nor

> "The Giant of the Band-beggars' Hall,
> The greatest Giant over them all."

"You're welcome," sez the Giant to the eagle. "It's so long since you were here I thought I'd never see your face more."

"It's seldom come the better," sez the eagle; "you'll never see it again if I have my will. And, indeed," sez he, "if it wasn't for this bag I was sent with to you, you wouldn't see me now. There it is," sez the eagle, "and good-bye."

So off he flew, and the Giant said to himself he wondered who would be sending a bag to him, or what was in it. So, taking out a big clasp-knife, he cut open the bag, and out my brave Jack steps, and——

"How do ye do," sez Jack, sez he, "the Giant of the Band-beggars' Hall, the greatest Giant over them all?"

Well, the Giant, when he caught a glimpse of Jack, was staggered and dumbfoundered.

"Well, Jack," sez he, at length, when he come to himself,

"ye're a most wonderful fellow. This bangs all ever I knew," sez he. "I surely thought that I had the better of you; but I see you were too clever by half for me. And I'll stand to my contract, for you deserve to have your life spared. And more than that," sez he, "I have a young daughter that I never intended to let marry—for I couldn't think to get a husband for her that would be to my liking, till I fell in with you—but now that I have met you and seen the uncommon clever man you are entirely, you can have her if she takes your fancy, with a heart and a half, and a handsome fortune."

Jack said nothing to this till he would see her, for he had a fancy that no matter what fortune she might have—and he suspected the fortune such a Giant could give with her would be no miss—he could find nicer girls in Ireland. But, och, when he saw the very first sight of her, the beauties of Ireland all flew out of his head, and he was head and ears in love with her at once, for the like of her for pure downright loveliness he never before laid his two eyes on. And when her father asked her what she thought of Jack, she couldn't contain herself, she was that much in love with him. So the thing was settled up at once, for Jack was thinking of his poor father and mother grieving for him at home, and couldn't delay. Then the Giant of the Band-beggars' Hall counted out to Jack, as a fortune with the beauty, a sword that the man who fought with it couldn't be beaten, and a loaf of bread that would never grow less no matter how much was cut off it, and a flask of whiskey that would never be emptied no matter how much was drunk from it, and a purse that would always be full no matter how much was taken out of it. He then gave them two wishing-caps that they had only to put them on their heads and wish to be any place, and they would be there. So they took the Giant's blessing, and putting their caps on their heads, wished to be at the oldest of the three brother Giant's house that helped Jack; and when they come there Jack gave him the sword, for he said he had no use for it, seeing there wasn't a man in Ireland he was afraid of. They then put on their caps and wished to be at the next Giant's; and when they come there, Jack gave him the loaf, for he said Ireland never yet knew want. Then, they put on the caps again, and wished to be at the first Giant's house that Jack fell in with, and when they came there, Jack gave him the flask of whiskey, for, he said, the rivers in Ireland flowed with it. He kept the purse for himself, saying that he could do good with it. They then put on their caps, and wished to be home in the King's Castle in Ireland; and home they were at once. And that was the reception was for them! And there was the joy and the rejoicing! And all the country was asked to the wedding. And such a spread of eating and drinking, and carousing, lasting for nine days, was never known in Ireland afore! But Jack first went on the bridge, and hooked the trout that put its tail to its nose, and winked its eye about at him, and he stuck that trout against the wall with a corker pin through its body for the nine days the feast lasted, till it saw all the rejoicement, and wriggled and twisted, and heartily repented having ever been unrespectful to Jack. From that day forward Jack fished to his heart's content off the bridge, and he caught no end of the trouts for they couldn't trick him any longer, and none of them ever afterwards wagged their tails out of the water at Jack, and himself and his beautiful wife lived happy ever after.

# A CATALOG OF SELECTED
# DOVER BOOKS
## IN ALL FIELDS OF INTEREST

# A CATALOG OF SELECTED DOVER
# BOOKS IN ALL FIELDS OF INTEREST

CONCERNING THE SPIRITUAL IN ART, Wassily Kandinsky. Pioneering work by father of abstract art. Thoughts on color theory, nature of art. Analysis of earlier masters. 12 illustrations. 80pp. of text. 5⅜ x 8½. 23411-8 Pa. $4.95

ANIMALS: 1,419 Copyright-Free Illustrations of Mammals, Birds, Fish, Insects, etc., Jim Harter (ed.). Clear wood engravings present, in extremely lifelike poses, over 1,000 species of animals. One of the most extensive pictorial sourcebooks of its kind. Captions. Index. 284pp. 9 x 12. 23766-4 Pa. $14.95

CELTIC ART: The Methods of Construction, George Bain. Simple geometric techniques for making Celtic interlacements, spirals, Kells-type initials, animals, humans, etc. Over 500 illustrations. 160pp. 9 x 12. (USO) 22923-8 Pa. $9.95

AN ATLAS OF ANATOMY FOR ARTISTS, Fritz Schider. Most thorough reference work on art anatomy in the world. Hundreds of illustrations, including selections from works by Vesalius, Leonardo, Goya, Ingres, Michelangelo, others. 593 illustrations. 192pp. 7⅛ x 10¼. 20241-0 Pa. $9.95

CELTIC HAND STROKE-BY-STROKE (Irish Half-Uncial from "The Book of Kells"): An Arthur Baker Calligraphy Manual, Arthur Baker. Complete guide to creating each letter of the alphabet in distinctive Celtic manner. Covers hand position, strokes, pens, inks, paper, more. Illustrated. 48pp. 8¼ x 11. 24336-2 Pa. $3.95

EASY ORIGAMI, John Montroll. Charming collection of 32 projects (hat, cup, pelican, piano, swan, many more) specially designed for the novice origami hobbyist. Clearly illustrated easy-to-follow instructions insure that even beginning papercrafters will achieve successful results. 48pp. 8¼ x 11. 27298-2 Pa. $3.50

THE COMPLETE BOOK OF BIRDHOUSE CONSTRUCTION FOR WOODWORKERS, Scott D. Campbell. Detailed instructions, illustrations, tables. Also data on bird habitat and instinct patterns. Bibliography. 3 tables. 63 illustrations in 15 figures. 48pp. 5¼ x 8½. 24407-5 Pa. $2.50

BLOOMINGDALE'S ILLUSTRATED 1886 CATALOG: Fashions, Dry Goods and Housewares, Bloomingdale Brothers. Famed merchants' extremely rare catalog depicting about 1,700 products: clothing, housewares, firearms, dry goods, jewelry, more. Invaluable for dating, identifying vintage items. Also, copyright-free graphics for artists, designers. Co-published with Henry Ford Museum & Greenfield Village. 160pp. 8¼ x 11. 25780-0 Pa. $10.95

HISTORIC COSTUME IN PICTURES, Braun & Schneider. Over 1,450 costumed figures in clearly detailed engravings–from dawn of civilization to end of 19th century. Captions. Many folk costumes. 256pp. 8⅜ x 11¾. 23150-X Pa. $12.95

## CATALOG OF DOVER BOOKS

STICKLEY CRAFTSMAN FURNITURE CATALOGS, Gustav Stickley and L. & J. G. Stickley. Beautiful, functional furniture in two authentic catalogs from 1910. 594 illustrations, including 277 photos, show settles, rockers, armchairs, reclining chairs, bookcases, desks, tables. 183pp. 6½ x 9¼.                     23838-5 Pa. $11.95

AMERICAN LOCOMOTIVES IN HISTORIC PHOTOGRAPHS: 1858 to 1949, Ron Ziel (ed.). A rare collection of 126 meticulously detailed official photographs, called "builder portraits," of American locomotives that majestically chronicle the rise of steam locomotive power in America. Introduction. Detailed captions. xi + 129pp. 9 x 12.                     27393-8 Pa. $12.95

AMERICA'S LIGHTHOUSES: An Illustrated History, Francis Ross Holland, Jr. Delightfully written, profusely illustrated fact-filled survey of over 200 American lighthouses since 1716. History, anecdotes, technological advances, more. 240pp. 8 x 10¾.
25576-X Pa. $12.95

TOWARDS A NEW ARCHITECTURE, Le Corbusier. Pioneering manifesto by founder of "International School." Technical and aesthetic theories, views of industry, economics, relation of form to function, "mass-production split" and much more. Profusely illustrated. 320pp. 6⅛ x 9¼. (USO)                     25023-7 Pa. $9.95

HOW THE OTHER HALF LIVES, Jacob Riis. Famous journalistic record, exposing poverty and degradation of New York slums around 1900, by major social reformer. 100 striking and influential photographs. 233pp. 10 x 7⅞.
22012-5 Pa. $11.95

FRUIT KEY AND TWIG KEY TO TREES AND SHRUBS, William M. Harlow. One of the handiest and most widely used identification aids. Fruit key covers 120 deciduous and evergreen species; twig key 160 deciduous species. Easily used. Over 300 photographs. 126pp. 5⅜ x 8½.                     20511-8 Pa. $3.95

COMMON BIRD SONGS, Dr. Donald J. Borror. Songs of 60 most common U.S. birds: robins, sparrows, cardinals, bluejays, finches, more–arranged in order of increasing complexity. Up to 9 variations of songs of each species.
Cassette and manual 99911-4 $8.95

ORCHIDS AS HOUSE PLANTS, Rebecca Tyson Northen. Grow cattleyas and many other kinds of orchids–in a window, in a case, or under artificial light. 63 illustrations. 148pp. 5⅜ x 8½.                     23261-1 Pa. $4.95

MONSTER MAZES, Dave Phillips. Masterful mazes at four levels of difficulty. Avoid deadly perils and evil creatures to find magical treasures. Solutions for all 32 exciting illustrated puzzles. 48pp. 8¼ x 11.                     26005-4 Pa. $2.95

MOZART'S DON GIOVANNI (DOVER OPERA LIBRETTO SERIES), Wolfgang Amadeus Mozart. Introduced and translated by Ellen H. Bleiler. Standard Italian libretto, with complete English translation. Convenient and thoroughly portable–an ideal companion for reading along with a recording or the performance itself. Introduction. List of characters. Plot summary. 121pp. 5¼ x 8½.
24944-1 Pa. $3.95

TECHNICAL MANUAL AND DICTIONARY OF CLASSICAL BALLET, Gail Grant. Defines, explains, comments on steps, movements, poses and concepts. 15-page pictorial section. Basic book for student, viewer. 127pp. 5⅜ x 8½.
21843-0 Pa. $4.95

AUTOBIOGRAPHY: The Story of My Experiments with Truth, Mohandas K. Gandhi. Boyhood, legal studies, purification, the growth of the Satyagraha (nonviolent protest) movement. Critical, inspiring work of the man responsible for the freedom of India. 480pp. 5⅜ x 8½. (USO)                     24593-4 Pa. $8.95

CELTIC MYTHS AND LEGENDS, T. W. Rolleston. Masterful retelling of Irish and Welsh stories and tales. Cuchulain, King Arthur, Deirdre, the Grail, many more. First paperback edition. 58 full-page illustrations. 512pp. 5⅜ x 8½.     26507-2 Pa. $9.95

THE PRINCIPLES OF PSYCHOLOGY, William James. Famous long course complete, unabridged. Stream of thought, time perception, memory, experimental methods; great work decades ahead of its time. 94 figures. 1,391pp. 5⅜ x 8½. 2-vol. set.
Vol. I: 20381-6 Pa. $13.95
Vol. II: 20382-4 Pa. $14.95

THE WORLD AS WILL AND REPRESENTATION, Arthur Schopenhauer. Definitive English translation of Schopenhauer's life work, correcting more than 1,000 errors, omissions in earlier translations. Translated by E. F. J. Payne. Total of 1,269pp. 5⅜ x 8½. 2-vol. set.               Vol. 1: 21761-2 Pa. $12.95
Vol. 2: 21762-0 Pa. $12.95

MAGIC AND MYSTERY IN TIBET, Madame Alexandra David-Neel. Experiences among lamas, magicians, sages, sorcerers, Bonpa wizards. A true psychic discovery. 32 illustrations. 321pp. 5⅜ x 8½. (USO)            22682-4 Pa. $9.95

THE EGYPTIAN BOOK OF THE DEAD, E. A. Wallis Budge. Complete reproduction of Ani's papyrus, finest ever found. Full hieroglyphic text, interlinear transliteration, word-for-word translation, smooth translation. 533pp. 6½ x 9¼.
21866-X Pa. $11.95

MATHEMATICS FOR THE NONMATHEMATICIAN, Morris Kline. Detailed, college-level treatment of mathematics in cultural and historical context, with numerous exercises. Recommended Reading Lists. Tables. Numerous figures. 641pp. 5⅜ x 8½.
24823-2 Pa. $11.95

THEORY OF WING SECTIONS: Including a Summary of Airfoil Data, Ira H. Abbott and A. E. von Doenhoff. Concise compilation of subsonic aerodynamic characteristics of NACA wing sections, plus description of theory. 350pp. of tables. 693pp. 5⅜ x 8½.                                   60586-8 Pa. $14.95

THE RIME OF THE ANCIENT MARINER, Gustave Doré, S. T. Coleridge. Doré's finest work; 34 plates capture moods, subtleties of poem. Flawless full-size reproductions printed on facing pages with authoritative text of poem. "Beautiful. Simply beautiful."–*Publisher's Weekly.* 77pp. 9¼ x 12.       22305-1 Pa. $7.95

NORTH AMERICAN INDIAN DESIGNS FOR ARTISTS AND CRAFTSPEOPLE, Eva Wilson. Over 360 authentic copyright-free designs adapted from Navajo blankets, Hopi pottery, Sioux buffalo hides, more. Geometrics, symbolic figures, plant and animal motifs, etc. 128pp. 8⅜ x 11. (EUK)           25341-4 Pa. $8.95

SCULPTURE: Principles and Practice, Louis Slobodkin. Step-by-step approach to clay, plaster, metals, stone; classical and modern. 253 drawings, photos. 255pp. 8⅛ x 11.
22960-2 Pa. $11.95

THE INFLUENCE OF SEA POWER UPON HISTORY, 1660–1783, A. T. Mahan. Influential classic of naval history and tactics still used as text in war colleges. First paperback edition. 4 maps. 24 battle plans. 640pp. 5⅜ x 8½. 25509-3 Pa. $14.95

THE STORY OF THE TITANIC AS TOLD BY ITS SURVIVORS, Jack Winocour (ed.). What it was really like. Panic, despair, shocking inefficiency, and a little heroism. More thrilling than any fictional account. 26 illustrations. 320pp. 5⅜ x 8½. 20610-6 Pa. $8.95

FAIRY AND FOLK TALES OF THE IRISH PEASANTRY, William Butler Yeats (ed.). Treasury of 64 tales from the twilight world of Celtic myth and legend: "The Soul Cages," "The Kildare Pooka," "King O'Toole and his Goose," many more. Introduction and Notes by W. B. Yeats. 352pp. 5⅜ x 8½. 26941-8 Pa. $8.95

BUDDHIST MAHAYANA TEXTS, E. B. Cowell and Others (eds.). Superb, accurate translations of basic documents in Mahayana Buddhism, highly important in history of religions. The Buddha-karita of Asvaghosha, Larger Sukhavativyuha, more. 448pp. 5⅜ x 8½. 25552-2 Pa. $12.95

ONE TWO THREE . . . INFINITY: Facts and Speculations of Science, George Gamow. Great physicist's fascinating, readable overview of contemporary science: number theory, relativity, fourth dimension, entropy, genes, atomic structure, much more. 128 illustrations. Index. 352pp. 5⅜ x 8½. 25664-2 Pa. $8.95

ENGINEERING IN HISTORY, Richard Shelton Kirby, et al. Broad, nontechnical survey of history's major technological advances: birth of Greek science, industrial revolution, electricity and applied science, 20th-century automation, much more. 181 illustrations. ". . . excellent . . ."–*Isis.* Bibliography. vii + 530pp. 5⅜ x 8¼. 26412-2 Pa. $14.95

DALÍ ON MODERN ART: The Cuckolds of Antiquated Modern Art, Salvador Dalí. Influential painter skewers modern art and its practitioners. Outrageous evaluations of Picasso, Cézanne, Turner, more. 15 renderings of paintings discussed. 44 calligraphic decorations by Dalí. 96pp. 5⅜ x 8½. (USO) 29220-7 Pa. $4.95

ANTIQUE PLAYING CARDS: A Pictorial History, Henry René D'Allemagne. Over 900 elaborate, decorative images from rare playing cards (14th–20th centuries): Bacchus, death, dancing dogs, hunting scenes, royal coats of arms, players cheating, much more. 96pp. 9¼ x 12¼. 29265-7 Pa. $12.95

MAKING FURNITURE MASTERPIECES: 30 Projects with Measured Drawings, Franklin H. Gottshall. Step-by-step instructions, illustrations for constructing handsome, useful pieces, among them a Sheraton desk, Chippendale chair, Spanish desk, Queen Anne table and a William and Mary dressing mirror. 224pp. 8⅛ x 11¼. 29338-6 Pa. $13.95

THE FOSSIL BOOK: A Record of Prehistoric Life, Patricia V. Rich et al. Profusely illustrated definitive guide covers everything from single-celled organisms and dinosaurs to birds and mammals and the interplay between climate and man. Over 1,500 illustrations. 760pp. 7½ x 10⅜. 29371-8 Pa. $29.95

*Prices subject to change without notice.*

Available at your book dealer or write for free catalog to Dept. GI, Dover Publications, Inc., 31 East 2nd St., Mineola, N.Y. 11501. Dover publishes more than 500 books each year on science, elementary and advanced mathematics, biology, music, art, literary history, social sciences and other areas.